Jayge ★

"YOU WANT FACTS, MR. WALLACH?" CHAMBRUN ASKED.

"Please," Wallach said.

"There is no gun anywhere in the health club. There is no indication where the actual shooting took place. The boy obviously bled profusely—pints and pints. If he was shot in the water there's no way to prove it out. The water circulates in the pool, and if the bleeding took place there, then only a few streaks of blood are left. There is no sign of the bullet, which obviously exited from the back of the boy's head. Those are the facts, Mr. Wallach—or you might say those are facts we don't have."

———————— ★ ————————

HUGH PENTECOST
WITH INTENT TO KILL

WORLDWIDE.

TORONTO · NEW YORK · LONDON · PARIS
AMSTERDAM · STOCKHOLM · HAMBURG
ATHENS · MILAN · TOKYO · SYDNEY

WITH INTENT TO KILL

A Worldwide Mystery/October 1991

First published by Dodd, Mead & Company, Inc.

ISBN 0-373-26081-4

PART ONE

ONE

As HE DID every morning of his life except Sundays, Carl Hulman arrived at work a few minutes before nine o'clock in the morning. His place of employment was on the fourteenth floor of the Hotel Beaumont, New York's top luxury hotel. Hulman was the day manager of the Health Club, a very busy place in the life of the Beaumont. There was locker-room space, a fully equipped gym, two squash courts, a swimming pool, massage tables, and resting areas over which sunlamps hovered. Once a customer had been through the mill there was a lounge where, still without dressing, he could be served fruit juices, or coffee, or even a short-order sandwich.

It was Carl Hulman's custom to arrive about fifteen minutes before the rest of the staff was expected on the job. He was a quiet-spoken perfectionist. After changing out of his street clothes and into chino pants, a white T-shirt, socks, and sneakers, he took a tour of his domain, pausing to turn on the power in the steam room. If the slightest thing was out of place or had been neglected by the night crew at close-up time, Hulman would spot it.

That morning everything was exactly as it should have been until he reached the swimming pool. He switched on the fluorescent lights and stepped out to the edge of the pool. There he stopped, taking in his breath in a sudden, sharp gasp. Floating in the pool was the fully clothed body of a man, arms and legs spread-eagled, smears of blood in the water around it. Hulman knew instantly that it was a body and not a living person. He had been a medic in the army for a couple of years in Vietnam. He moved closer, squatting down on the edge of the pool. He knew a gunshot wound when he saw one, and there was what he guessed was an exit wound at the back of the dead man's head. The dead man had been shot in the forehead or face.

Hulman went quickly to the nearest phone. This was a job for Jerry Dodd, chief of the Beaumont's security force.

THE BEAUMONT IS FAMOUS for a number of things, perhaps most notably its legendary manager, Pierre Chambrun. The French-born Chambrun, who could have been played to a tee by that late great actor Claude Rains, is short, stocky, and elegant in his movements. His dark eyes are buried behind deep pouches and they can twinkle with humor, grow warm with compassion, or turn cold as a hanging judge's. His clothes are custom tailored, his shirts, ties, and shoes made to order. He is something of a Beau Brummell but he handles it without affectation.

Some of us who work for Chambrun believe he is equipped with some kind of magical radar system that makes it possible for him to detect a malfunction in the Swiss-watch working of the world over which he presides almost before it happens. He is, of course, the king, the mayor, the boss of a small city within a city. He operates his own police force, a shopping center, restaurants and bars, a bank, the Health Club, living quarters for a thousand guests, hospital facilities, game rooms, banquet halls. Unfortunately, Chambrun can't change human nature. He can't eliminate greed, or jealousy, or a passion for revenge, or the impulse toward treachery and betrayal in the individual man or woman. And so, as in every other place on earth, these ugly psychoses erupt in Chambrun's world, dislocating his best efforts toward peace and order. It was one of these dark and twisted impulses that presented Carl Hulman with a dead man in the swimming pool.

I was with Chambrun in his second-floor office that morning when he got the word that there was a "problem" in the Health Club. Chambrun's office is more like an elegant living room than a place of business. He sits at a carved Florentine desk with a blue-period Picasso, a gift from the artist himself, staring crookedly down at him from the opposite wall. The beautiful Oriental rug on the floor was a gift from some Middle Eastern potentate for whom Chambrun had done some special service during a stay at the Beaumont. The chairs and tables, the couch, are comfortable but priceless antiques.

Chambrun lives by rigid routines at certain times of the day. The early morning is one of these times. He arrives at his office from his penthouse on the roof at precisely eight o'clock. Betsy Ruysdale, his incompa-

rable secretary, greets him in the outer office. In the
private office Claude Boucher, assistant to the master
chef, waits with a gourmet breakfast. It is always
hearty because the Great Man will not eat again until
the evening hour. The main dish, after juice, may
consist of a filet mignon with hash-browned pota-
toes, or brook trout, or a ham steak, or shad roe, or
lamb chops. The rest never varies: gluten toast, sweet
butter, a variety of jams and marmalades, and two
cups of American coffee. The rest of the day he
drinks, constantly, a foul-tasting Turkish coffee, which
Betsy Ruysdale prepares for him in a special coffee
maker on the Burmese sideboard.

For an hour Ruysdale guards him with her life
against anything including fire, flood, tornado—perhaps even murder. At precisely nine o'clock I, Mark
Haskell, in charge of public relations for the hotel, am
ushered into the Presence to start the day's business.
Chambrun, at his desk by then, has the registration
cards from the day and night before. He and Ruysdale and I go over them. Our guests might have been
surprised had they known of the information that appears on those cards. There is, not unexpectedly, a
credit rating. But there are other symbols that tell us
whether the guest, man or woman, is an alcoholic, a
man-chaser or a woman-chaser, gay, lesbian, a man
cheating on a wife or a wife cheating on a husband.
We are close to the United Nations and many of our
guests come from other parts of the world. The cards
will reveal where they are from, their politics, their
business. There is sometimes another symbol, which

indicates that Chambrun knows something special about the guests he doesn't want made available to the rest of the staff. That whole file on guests would have been worth a billion dollars to a professional black-mailer.

There are usually a few wisecracks as we go over those cards each morning. "Here's old so-and-so again" is the way it goes. "We'd better tell the maid on the twenty-fourth floor to wear her chastity belt!" My reason for being there has to do with serving the guests properly. A Hollywood celebrity may want to be in town incognito, without fanfare, or he may want the word spread that he is in town, probably to promote a film, or a television series, or even a book. My job is to keep him hidden or blow a horn, depending on his desires.

One of the phones rang on Chambrun's desk—I say "rang" but it's really just a silent, blinking light. Betsy Ruysdale picked it up and answered. She handed the phone to Chambrun. "It's Jerry Dodd," she said. "Some kind of emergency."

Chambrun took the phone. "Yes, Jerry?" I saw that cold, angry look take over his face that happens when something has upset orderly routines. He put down the phone.

"We may have a homicide up in the Health Club," he told us. "Let's move it, Mark."

ABNORMALITY HAD already taken over when Chambrun and I reached the fourteenth floor. One of Jerry Dodd's men was guarding the entrance to the Health

Club with half a dozen of Carl Hulman's daytime staff barred from reporting for work as usual.

"What's the story, Alec?" Chambrun asked Jerry Dodd's man. He knows everyone's first name who works for the Beaumont and uses it unless you are out of favor. The only last name he uses consistently is Betsy Ruysdale's. He neuters her by simply calling her "Ruysdale," although rumor has it that she plays a more intimate role in his life than that of secretary and executive assistant.

"Gunshot homicide, Mr. Chambrun," Alec Watson told Chambrun. "Jerry wants everyone kept out until the homicide cops get here. That doesn't mean you, of course."

"And Mark," Chambrun said.

Alec Watson let us in.

We walked through the deserted gym and the massage room to the pool. Jerry Dodd and Carl Hulman were at the far end looking down at the body in the water. Jerry Dodd, our security chief, is a slim, wiry, intense little man, tougher than nails, whom Chambrun stole away from the FBI some years back to protect his world.

We joined them. I wasn't sure my breakfast was going to stay put when I looked down at the gaping hole in the back of the dead man's head.

"We haven't touched anything, boss," Jerry said. "Carl found him when he was opening up. Carl was an army medic, you know. He saw there was nothing he could do for him and called me."

"Small little man," I heard myself say.

"More likely a young boy," Chambrun said. "Sneakers, Levi jeans, sports shirt."

"Somebody sure didn't like him," Jerry Dodd said. "Shot in the face with something like a cannon."

"Why here?" It was a typical Chambrun question. He wasn't, as yet, concerned with the identity of the victim or the murderer. A violence here meant police, and reporters, and an unwelcome spotlight on his beloved hotel.

Nobody answered Chambrun's question because at that moment we were invaded by the men from Homicide. Lieutenant Hardy, the man in charge, could be called an old friend of Chambrun's. He was a big, blond man who reminded me more of a professional football linebacker than a highly efficient detective.

Hardy gave Chambrun a tight little smile. "So you've staged another one, Pierre," he said.

There have been murders at the Beaumont. As I've said, it is a city within a city. What happens in the metropolis outside its walls also happens inside them. Stationed in the area that includes the Beaumont, Hardy had found himself in Chambrun's world rather more frequently than he was welcome. He and Chambrun were totally different and yet complementary to each other. Hardy is a dogged collector of detail, Chambrun a brilliant hunch player. Chambrun came up with intuitive answers way ahead of his friend, but it was Hardy who gathered the evidence and proved out Chambrun's theories. Together they had so far been an unbeatable team. Whoever was responsible for the victim in the pool had better be on his way to some far corner of the earth, I thought.

When Hardy's people, after taking many photographs, lifted the body out of the pool and laid it, face up, on the tile floor I wished I had gone somewhere else. There was, in fact, almost no face to look at. The victim had been hit by some kind of expanding bullet that had obliterated the forehead and eyes. The lower half of the face, drained of blood, fish-belly white, looked strangely out of shape like something in a funhouse mirror.

Hardy, kneeling beside the body, touched the chin with the tips of his fingers.

"Hadn't started to shave yet," he muttered. "Can't be over thirteen, fourteen years old."

One of Hardy's men went through the pockets of the waterlogged pants and the patch pocket on the sports shirt.

"Couple of dollar bills and some change," the detective reported. "And this." He held up a folded slip of green paper he'd found in the shirt pocket. "No I.D."

"A kid wouldn't be carrying a driver's license or a Social Security card," Hardy said. He scowled at the green slip of paper and handed it to Chambrun. I knew what it was without looking.

For twenty-four hours, from midnight to midnight the night before, there had been a telethon held in the ballroom of the hotel to raise money for cancer research. It was an annual event, presided over by Stan Nelson, the popular singing star who is today's version of the earlier Vallee, Crosby, or Sinatra. The green slip was a pledge card you could fill out with your name, address, phone number, and the amount you wanted to give.

"Not filled out," Chambrun said. He turned it over and his frown deepened. On the back of the card, blurred slightly by exposure to the water, was a handwritten message. *"With best wishes and lots of good luck. Stan Nelson."*

Chambrun handed the slip back to Hardy so that the detective could read the message.

"Every year Stan Nelson holds a telethon here for cancer research," he said. "Midnight to midnight. He picked up over a million dollars this last time— Thursday night to Friday night. Thousands of people turn up to hear him sing, to kick in something or pledge something. Jerry Lewis does the same kind of thing for muscular dystrophy. This is a pledge card. This kid evidently used it to get Stan Nelson's autograph."

"But no pledge, so no name."

"Unfortunately no name."

"Could Nelson know him?" Hardy asked.

"Not likely, I should think," Chambrun said. "Hundreds of kids along with genuine donors asking for autographs."

"It could be worth a try," Hardy said. "You have any idea where Nelson might be located?"

"He's probably sound asleep in his suite on the thirty-fifth floor," Chambrun said. "Twenty-four hours without any sleep takes some catching up."

"We better get him down here to take a look," Hardy said.

"The switchboard undoubtedly has orders not to put through a call till sometime this afternoon," Chambrun said.

"So cancel the order," Hardy said. "We have a homicide here, Pierre."

Chambrun glanced at me. "Go up to Stan Nelson's suite, Mark. He has his own bodyguard and that accompanist of his staying with him. One of them might know this kid. I don't like to rouse a man who's just raised a million dollars for charity. He's entitled to recover."

"Bodyguard?" Hardy asked, his eyebrows raised.

"Thousands of screaming freaks trying to get at him every day of his life," Chambrun said. "In this crazy world we live in, Walter, who knows when one of them may turn out not to like music?"

TWO

THIS IS PARTLY A STORY about one of the most popular men in America, Stan Nelson. I like music and I've been a fan of Stan Nelson's for a long time. When I say I like music I don't mean I like rock or country music, where the same phrase and the same lyrics are repeated over and over.

> *Mamma, I gotta tell you it hurts,*
> *Mamma, I gotta tell you it hurts,*
> *Mamma, I gotta tell you it hurts,*
> *It hurts, it hurts, it hurts.*

After a while you get the idea that "it hurts." Stan Nelson has stuck all his career to the songs I first heard when I was growing up—the tunes of Cole Porter, and Gershwin, and Duke Ellington, and Rodgers and Hammerstein, and Irving Berlin. That period. The melody and the lyrics when Stan worked with them were clean, and warm, and romantic—and witty when wit was called for. I know girls screamed at Crosby and Sinatra the way they do at Stan Nelson, which proves, I guess, that his kind of music can still compete with a bearded slob with an electric guitar, or someone with a swiveling pelvis like Presley or a Tom Jones.

Over the past few years since the cancer telethon
began to be held at the Beaumont I've come to know
Stan Nelson in a casual way. It is my job to greet him
when he arrives, make sure that everything is the way
he wants it in his private suite and in the ballroom
where he'll do what I think of as his man-killing marathon for charity. He is a quiet, pleasant guy with no
apparent sharp edges to him. In his early forties, he
still has a boyish quality to him, with his reddish-
brown hair worn a little longer than short, and a little
shorter than long. His eyes are a sleepy blue with a
suggestion of vulnerability in them. I suppose that
may explain why girls—and women—go for him so
hard. He needs something and they want to give it.

In his early days I guess Stan Nelson cut quite a
swathe in Hollywood. He sang in a movie, a second-
ary part, and he was a star overnight. That's when the
women thing started. He was linked with quite a few
glamorous names, and the gossip ladies had a field day
with him. Eventually there was some kind of scandal
about a live-in pal, who sued him for what is known
today as palimony. The lady lost her case in court.
And then the female segment of the population went
into mourning. Stan Nelson married a girl who had no
connection with show business. It changed his image
but not at the cost of his career. It was apparently a
perfect marriage, there were two children—a girl and
a boy—and he became the ideal husband to the
women who idolized him.

A half-dozen films had been blockbusters, and he
had a hatful of gold records, he cleaned up in Vegas

and Atlantic City. This was the all-American boy grown into the all-American success. He was the all-American Mr. Nice Guy.

As far as I know Stan comes to New York only once a year for the cancer thing. His wife, Ellen, doesn't make these trips with him so I have never met her or the two kids, now ten and eight. He showed me pictures of the kids, like any proud papa. They were dolls, little blond dolls.

Stan Nelson did not, however, travel alone. In this day and age of drug-ridden crazies people with any fame at all are targets for psyched-out freaks. The president of the United States is the victim of a young man who wants to create a macho image of himself to impress a young actress he has never met. John Lennon of Beatle fame is shot down in cold blood by a kid he never met, never knew, who was apparently not a member of any cause.

"Half the women in the world are in love with Stan, which means that all their husbands and boyfriends are jealous of him and hate his guts," Butch Mancuso told me once, to explain his presence.

Butch is Stan Nelson's permanent bodyguard. He has patterned his own image after the late George Raft—shiny, patent-leather black hair, narrowed dark eyes, swift and agile as a cat. Threaten Stan in any way and you were facing death when Butch Mancuso stepped between you and his man. Butch was pleasant enough when he was sure of you. He liked to joke. He collected wisecracks from the best comics. He wasn't much of a drinking companion because he didn't drink.

"I have to be on the ball around the clock," he told me.

The other part of what you might call Stan Nelson's shadow was Johnny Floyd. Johnny's whole life, until Stan came into the picture, had been at a piano, playing in cheap saloons and nightclubs, and in second-rate jazz bands. He is egg-bald, perpetually angry, chain-smoking cigarettes. A hacking cough suggested that emphysema is in his not-too-distant future. Somewhere, early on, he had become the then unknown Stan Nelson's accompanist. He knew the ropes in the second-rate music world and he became a sort of manager for Stan, getting him jobs so they could both keep eating. Then, overnight, Stan was a big success and he didn't need Johnny anymore. But Mr. Nice Guy never turned away from this first good friend. Johnny still worked out new numbers with Stan, wrote his arrangements, and advised him on his career whether or not he needed advice. Butch Mancuso would have shot you between the eyes if you'd threatened Stan, Johnny Floyd would have torn you to pieces with his bare hands.

These two permanent fixtures were, I knew, sharing suite 35C with Stan while he caught up on sleep after his cancer show. I didn't think there was the slightest chance that Stan or Butch or Johnny would be any use to Lieutenant Hardy, but checking out on that autograph, written on the back of a green pledge card, was the kind of detail Hardy would never by-pass.

It was going on ten-thirty in the morning when I rang the doorbell at 35C. Butch Mancuso, who could have had no more sleep than Stan, opened the door before I could ring a second time. He was sleek, shaved, dressed, ready for another day. It is true he hadn't sung thirty-five or forty numbers during the marathon, answered telephone calls from donors, signed autographs. He had just stood by, occasionally stroking the butt of the gun he carried in a holster under his left arm, his dark eyes searching a thousand faces for trouble.

"Oh, it's you," he said. "The boss is sacked out, as if you didn't know."

"We've got trouble downstairs in the Health Club," I said. I told him what the trouble was.

"Stan can't help them," Butch said. "He must have signed a thousand autographs during the show. He wouldn't know one from another."

"Lieutenant Hardy needs him to say that he doesn't know this one," I said. "Chambrun persuaded him to let me come after Stan, so he wouldn't be dragged out of bed by some cop and taken down there before he was decently awake."

"Let 'em try," Butch said.

"You can't stop them, Butch, if that's the way they want it," I said.

Johnny Floyd joined us at that point. He was na-ked except for a pair of pajama pants. His pale blue eyes looked as if they were still half glued together, but the first cigarette of the day was already bobbing up and down between his thin lips.

"You guys got to shout?" he asked Butch and me.

I told him what was cooking.

"Christ Almighty!" Johnny said. "Stan will have to face cameras, reporters."

"I can take him down in the service elevator," I said. "He won't have to see anyone but the cops—and the body."

"It can't wait?"

"I'm afraid not, Johnny."

"Okay. I'll get him." He turned and disappeared down the corridor to the suite's bedrooms.

"A guy tries to do something good for people and they won't even let him have his sleep," Butch said. "This dead guy doesn't have any I.D.?"

"No. Only a green pledge card on which Stan signed his name."

"That had to be before midnight," Butch said. "That's damn near eleven hours ago. How did this kid get into the Health Club? They don't leave it open, do they?"

"They may have found that out by the time we get down there," I said.

THE OPERATION of a complex business like the Beaumont involves a mass of detailed routines that are not allowed to vary by so much as a hair. People work in shifts, and you do not miss your appointed time by even a matter of seconds. There are shifts of maids, of housekeepers, of maintenance people, bellhops, the front desk, bartenders, waiters, cooks and kitchen help, maitre d's, the business office, the telephone switchboards, the clean-up people, the security staff— and on and on. Chambrun and Miss Ruysdale, Jerry Dodd and I, are the only people who are available at any time of the day or night. Sometimes I wonder if I can remember what New York looks like I get out into the outer city so infrequently.

The Health Club operates with only two shifts. Carl Hulman comes in at just before nine with his crew of massage people, gym crew, squash professional, and a swimming instructor and lifeguard for the pool. At five o'clock the second shift headed by Tony Camargo, a bright young Italian, takes over. The beginning of that shift, next to the lunch hour, is the busiest time in the club; men headed home from work go through the exercises routines for the benefit of their health, and usually end up in one of the bars undoing it all with a few martinis.

Tony Camargo started out in the Beaumont as a bellboy on the night shift. Mike Maggio, the night bell captain, is some kind of distant relative and he brought Tony into the fold about ten years ago. The move to the Health Club was a step up the ladder that I suspect Tony wished that morning he hadn't taken.

Lieutenant Hardy wasn't tough with Tony, but he was persistent. The body of the murdered boy was covered with a tarpaulin now, still at the edge of the pool, and Tony couldn't take his eyes off it as Hardy went about his interrogation.

"Let's go over your routine, Camargo, from top to bottom," the detective said.

Tony was still in shock from having been asked to look at the blown away face of the dead boy. He moistened his lips as though they wouldn't work without help.

"I come in about a quarter to five," he said, his voice unsteady. "I check out with Carl Hulman here. There may be special instructions. It's all written down on the clipboard he carries. Someone may be asleep in the rest room and needs to be called at a certain time; a telephone message for someone we expect will be in later. Stuff like that."

"Was there anything special last night?"

"No. Regular routine stuff. The sheet's still on the clipboard. You can see for yourself."

"Your regular customers—your shift—start to come in just after five o'clock?"

"That's right. Lot of the Madison Avenue advertising people."

"Can anyone come in and make use of the facilities?"

"No, sir. You have to be registered in the hotel, or you have to be a member."

"Member?"

"A lot of people are regular customers of the hotel who aren't living here," Tony explained. "They use the bars and the restaurants and things like that. They pay a hundred bucks to be a Health Club member. You can't just walk in off the street, if that's what you're asking."

"That's what I'm asking," Hardy glanced down at the covered body. "He got in."

"Not while I was on!" Tony said. "We don't have any kid members. Oh, sometimes a boy like that might be registered in the hotel with his parents and he might be here to work out in the gym or swim in the pool. But not yesterday. There wasn't any kid like that in here during my shift last night."

"You're positive?"

"Positive. Whoever was here is listed on the clipboard. You can see for yourself everyone who checked in last night."

"You could slip up if the place was real busy."

Tony glanced at Chambrun who was standing a little way off. "You only slip up once when you're working for Mr. Chambrun," he said. "I've been working in the hotel for ten years, six years at this job. No slip-ups or I wouldn't be here."

"Take me to the end of your shift—when you close up," Hardy said.

"At nine-thirty there's a bell that sounds everywhere on this floor," Tony said. "That warns the customers that they have a half an hour to shower, get dressed, and get out."

"So everybody is gone by ten o'clock?"

"Or a minute or two after. Some of the older customers may dawdle a little."

"Last night?"

"Right on the button," Tony said. "I know, because I—I had a date later on and I was watching the clock."

"So at ten o'clock you went home?"

"Oh, gee, no, Lieutenant," Tony said. "Getting rid of the people is only the beginning of closing up. Me and my crew have to pick up—discarded towels, sheets from the massage room and rest rooms—all that kind of stuff has to go into the big laundry hampers and out into the service area. A special clean-up gang comes in and the whole place is scrubbed down from top to bottom. The pool is drained, and—"

"The pool is *drained?*" Hardy interrupted.

"Yes, sir. Drained, washed down with a high-powered hose, scrubbed out with power brushes. Then it's refilled, with the chlorine stuff they use added."

"You stayed for all that last night?"

"Every night, Lieutenant. It's damn near midnight before I get to leave. After all that cleanup is done we set up for Carl in the morning; clean towels in all the places they're supposed to go, clean sheets in the massage and rest rooms, gym equipment all in place. All Carl has to do in the morning is open the door and let the people in."

"After we've checked out to make sure the night crew has done everything they're supposed to do," Carl Hulman said. "Everything was in order this morning, except for that." He gestured toward the tarpaulin without looking.

"So you checked out last night, Camargo," Hardy said.

"Yes, sir."

"You checked out the pool?"

"Yes, sir."

"You're telling me this dead boy wasn't floating in the water then?"

"Of course he wasn't! I'd have been screaming for help if he was, wouldn't I?"

"You do this final checkout by yourself?"

"As a matter of fact Jimmy Heath, my assistant, usually walks the rounds with me."

"But last night—?"

"Jimmy was with me."

"So you've checked out, everything is done. What then?"

"There are five fire exits out of this place," Tony said. "I make sure all those are locked."

"The fire doors are all locked with iron bars," Jerry Dodd interrupted. "No way to open them from the outside when the bars are in place."

"I unlock them when I make my first round in the morning," Carl Hulman said.

"So you've locked the fire doors. What next?" Hardy asked.

"I go out the front," Tony said. "We've got a little short-order kitchen out there where we make coffee and stuff. Jimmy Heath and I go there to make sure all the electric appliances are turned off. That's the short-order cook's job before he leaves, but we check him out."

"Then?"

"Then we go to the front door, set the locks, pull 'em closed—and that's that."

"Set the locks?"

"They're Yale-type locks. You release them, pull the doors closed, and they're locked. Jimmy and I test the doors from the outside to make sure the locks have caught—and then we go."

"And they were locked when you left last night?"

"Yes, sir. That's for sure."

"You haven't mentioned turning off any lights."

"Oh! Well, when Jimmy and I make our last round we turn off the lights in each area as we leave it. The last light switches are just by the front door."

"You don't have keys in case you needed to get back in? Like you forgot something?"

"Oh, there are keys, Lieutenant. Two, for those two locks on the front door. They're on a wire ring with a big plastic tag on it. Carl Hulman leaves them for me in our little office. I take them when I leave and drop them with Mr. Nevers at the front desk in the lobby."

"Where they're locked up in a special key safe in the office," Jerry Dodd said. "Hulman gets them there in the morning when he comes in. And just so you don't waste time with it, Lieutenant, those front doors weren't forced. First thing I checked."

Hardy was silent for a moment. "So obviously this kid was hiding somewhere when you closed up," he said, finally.

"No way, Lieutenant," Camargo said.

"If there was no way he could get in after you locked up he must have been inside when you left. Could he hide in one of the lockers where your customers hang their clothes when they undress to exercise?"

"There aren't lockers in the real sense," Tony said. "Just little cubicles with coat hooks and hangers. They're wide open. Jimmy and I checked as usual, in case some customer went off and left his watch, or wallet, or a ring or something."

"And you did that last night?"

"Sure. Clean as a whistle last night."

"Linen closets?"

"No, sir. There are just open shelves for the clean stuff."

Chambrun spoke for the first time. "And two people had to hide, Walter. The boy didn't shoot himself, you know. No gun. You've looked everywhere. What we've got here, friend, is a classic locked-room mystery."

"To which there is always a perfectly simple answer if you look for it," Hardy said.

It was then that Stan Nelson and I came in, with Butch Mancuso and Johnny Floyd behind us.

MR. NICE GUY HADN'T MADE any complaint about answering the summons from Lieutenant Hardy. He could always go back to bed, he told me. But he took his time getting ready. It was a professional axiom that Stan Nelson didn't appear anywhere looking less than all put together. He shaved and showered and then put in a long distance all to his home in Beverly Hills. It must have been about eight o'clock in the morning out there. Then he dressed, casual but perfect; pale blue summer-weight slacks, a navy blue sports shirt, a seersucker jacket, navy blue socks and tan loafers.

What the well-dressed gentleman wears on a casual summer Saturday.

We ducked running into the public, as I'd promised, by using the service elevator which took us down to fourteen without encountering anyone but the cop guarding the rear entrance of the club.

"Seen you often, enjoyed your work," Lieutenant Hardy said when I introduced them.

Butch Mancuso and Johnny Floyd had to be explained and Stan stepped over to speak to Chambrun while that was going on.

"Not a pleasant sight, Mr. Nelson," Hardy said. He bent down and pulled the tarpaulin back from the dead boy.

"Jesus!" I heard Butch Mancuso say.

Stan Nelson looked down steadily for a moment and then turned away. "Some kind of expanding bullet?" he asked Hardy.

"Heavy caliber at least," Hardy said. "We haven't found the bullet so we have no ballistics report."

"Still in his skull?" Stan suggested.

"If I turned him over you'd see why I know it isn't," Hardy said. "Exit wound you could drive a truck through. You don't know him, Mr. Nelson?"

Stan shook his head, slowly. "Hard to be positive, with that wound, wouldn't you say?"

"About fourteen or fifteen years old."

"You might say I know thousands of fourteen-, fifteen-year-old kids," Stan said. "But I don't really know them. There were hundreds of them at the cancer telethon last night."

Hardy took a green pledge card out of his wallet and handed it to Stan. "This one was evidently there."

Stan nodded but made no comment.

"*'With best wishes and lots of good luck. Stan Nelson.'* You wrote that, Mr. Nelson?"

"I'd have to say so. It gets to be almost like a rubber stamp after you've written thousands of them."

"You didn't write his name on it. *'For so-and-so.'*"

"I gave that up long ago," Stan said. "Italian names, Polish names, even Chinese and Russian. I'd have to stop and get them to spell it out for me, and even then I'd botch it up. So I just write the same thing on every card—*'With best wishes and lots of good luck.'*"

"He didn't pledge anything, write his own name on it," Hardy said.

"If he pledged anything he'd have to turn the card in," Stan said. "Kids pick up a second card if they're looking for an autograph."

Hardy recovered the body and straightened up. "Thanks for your time, Mr. Nelson. I had to be sure."

Just then one of his plainclothes cops came up and took the lieutenant aside.

"How did the boy get in here?" Stan asked Chambrun.

"That's the jackpot question at the moment," Chambrun said. "How did the telethon do last night?"

"Nearly a million and a quarter," Stan said. "Best ever. I wanted to thank you for seeing to it that everything ran so smoothly. I'd have looked you up later to say so."

"My job," Chambrun said.

I could tell his mind wasn't on pleasantries or courtesies.

Hardy and his plainclothesman rejoined us. The lieutenant's face had a curious, tight look to it that hadn't been there before. "This is Sergeant Schroeder, Mr. Nelson," he said, introducing the other cop. "The sergeant's been monitoring the phone for us in the front office. This is going to be a jolt or a bad joke for you, Mr. Nelson. An anonymous caller, male, informed Sergeant Schroeder that the dead boy we found in the pool is your son."

Stan gave the lieutenant a blank, unresponsive look. "I don't get it," he said.

"That's exactly what he said, Mr. Nelson," Schroeder said. "'The dead boy you found in the pool is Stan Nelson's son.'"

"Well, it's a bad joke, Lieutenant," Stan said. "I do have a son. His name is Bobby. He's eight years old. He's in California. I spoke to him on the phone five minutes before I came down here."

"Some coked-up freak trying to get in the act," Johnny Floyd said, his eyes narrowed against the smoke from his cigarette. "Happens to us all the time."

"The thing about this is that we haven't given out a word about this yet to the press or the media. There isn't any way for anyone on the outside to know what's happened here."

"Except someone who knows," Chambrun said. "There is someone who knows, Walter. The man who fired the shot."

But it turned out there were others. Another of Hardy's cops joined us. "There's a phone call for Mr. Haskell," he said. "He says he's Eliot Stevens of International Press."

Stevens is a reporter with whom I have a good relationship. He would be calling me to chat about the weather. I glanced at Chambrun and Hardy, asking without words for instructions.

"This thing has leaked, Lieutenant," the new cop said. "Reporters, photographers, the TV people in the lobby and outside this place in the corridor. They want to know is it true the victim is Stan Nelson's son."

"Damn!" Hardy said.

"It seems our anonymous friend has been busy," Chambrun said.

IN MY JOB AT THE BEAUMONT the press can wear two hats. If we have a story we want to publicize they can be our friends. If there is something we want to keep under cover they can be the enemy. Right now we had nothing to give them except the fact of a murder, not who the victim was or who was responsible for his death, or why. Mr. Anonymous was way ahead of us with his phony rumor that the dead boy was Stan Nelson's son. But that was enough to provide the media with a scandalous field day unless we could put a stop to it.

"We can't have an army in here," Hardy said. "We've got to go over every inch of this place without interference."

"They know Homicide isn't here for a picnic," Chambrun said. "You better see them, Walter. Tell them you have no facts yet."

"And, for God's sake, tell them I don't have a son this age," Stan Nelson said. "I never laid eyes on this dead boy before."

"Except when you signed an autograph for him, Mr. Nelson," Hardy said.

"He's one of a jumble of hundreds of faces," Stan said.

I suggested we let Eliot Stevens in. He could be trusted. He might help turn off the garbage about the dead boy being Stan's son. Eliot could be counted on to sit on a story if he knew he was going to get it all on the level when the time came to break it.

Chambrun agreed with me.

I went out to the telephone in the office where Eliot was waiting patiently on the other end of the line.

"I was just about to give up on you, chum," he said.

"Look," I said, "we've got a murder up here. The victim *isn't* Stan Nelson's son. Where did you get that?"

"Anonymous phone call," Eliot said. "Every newspaper, radio and TV station has had the same call."

"Can you get away from the rest of them and come up on the service elevator? Hardy's waiting. He'll send a cop down to bring you up. You'll have to hang on to what you get till we give you the green light."

"Is Stan Nelson there with you?"

"Yes."

"Will he talk?"

"He'll tell you the dead boy is a stranger to him."

"I don't want to wind up running behind the rest of this gang, Mark."

"A promise," I said.

"Send down your guide dog," he said.

Eliot Stevens is slender, sandy-haired, looking amiably professorial behind owlish, horn-rimmed glasses. He is, however, just about the sharpest investigative reporter I've come across in my experience, and I've had dealings with quite a few of them in my time at the Beaumont. Eliot will never have to give back a Pulitzer prize for having faked a story. When he goes into print you can depend on it that his facts are facts. Rumor is rumor until he can nail it down for truth.

One of Hardy's men went down to the lobby level in the service elevator to pick up Eliot. I met him when he came up the back way to the Health Club. While we walked through the gym and the massage room toward the pool I gave him the bare bones; Hulman's discovery of the body, the bullet that exited from the back of the boy's head not yet found, no gun, no I.D. Just the green pledge card on which Stan Nelson had signed his autograph.

"This crazy on the phone who says the dead boy is Stan's son is full of it," I said. "Stan has two kids, a daughter ten, a son eight, both alive and well and with his wife in Beverly Hills.''

"Nobody alerted Missing Persons? Nobody asking the cops to find a lost boy?" Eliot asked.

"If anyone has it hasn't gotten to Hardy yet," I said.

We reached the pool. Chambrun, Hardy, and Stan Nelson were standing in one group; Butch Mancuso, Johnny Floyd, and Tony Camargo in another. Carl Hulman wasn't there any longer. Hardy's men were going over the whole area like busy insects. Eliot is well known to Chambrun and Hardy.

"You understand whatever you see or hear is off the record till I say so, Eliot," Hardy said.

"Until you keep something back from me, Lieutenant," Eliot said with his gentle smile.

I introduced Eliot to Stan.

"Nice to meet you, Stan," Eliot said. "The man who outlasted rock music. I bless you for that. You helped keep something alive that's worth hearing."

"There are others who deserve your blessing," Stan said. "Sinatra, Tony Bennett, Mel Tormé, Peggy Lee, Sarah Vaughan, Steve Lawrence and Eydie Gorme."

"Fun to talk about it sometime," Eliot said. He turned back to Hardy. "Do I get to view the remains, Lieutenant?"

Hardy bent down and pulled back the tarpaulin from the dead boy's mangled face.

"Oh, wow!" Eliot said. He looked away quickly. "His own mother wouldn't know him."

The canvas went back over the body.

"You signed an autograph for him, Stan?" Eliot asked.

"And a hundred others like him," Stan said. "The thing I'm most interested in making clear to you, Stevens, is that he's a total stranger to me. I didn't sign an autograph for anyone I knew, or I'd remember. He isn't, for God sake, my son. I have two kids: Kathy, ten, and Bobby, eight. That's my total score."

Eliot fished a cigarette out of his pocket and held his lighter to it. "You and I met before, Stan, but there's no reason you should remember it."

"Oh?" Stan said.

"Was it nineteen sixty-eight? California. Some broad was suing you for what we now call 'palimony.' Been living with you for a couple of years. She lost the suit. That was before some smart lawyers found a way to make a profit from that kind of case."

"Oh, God," Stan said.

"Her name was Nora Sands, as I remember it," Eliot said.

"It wasn't a secret then. I hoped it was forgotten about now," Stan said. "I've been very happily married for eleven years, I have a family. Nora Sands is a bad dream I'd almost forgotten."

"I was in a group of reporters who interviewed you after the trial," Eliot said.

"So what does that have to do with the price of eggs?" Hardy asked. "We've got work to do, Eliot."

Eliot was looking steadily at Stan. "The Hollywood gossip ladies had some fun with that case for a while, didn't they, Stan? Nora Sands had an infant son when she brought suit against you. A lot of people at the time thought it might be your kid, as I remember."

"Oh, God save us!" Stan said. "Yes, yes, yes! There was talk. Nora never claimed I was the kid's father. If she had she might have collected from me. After all, we *did* live together for two years, and her baby was born a few months after we broke up."

"So?"

"You covered the trial?"

"Yes."

"Then you know I was making a film—on location for about ten days. I came home unexpectedly one night and found her in the hay—in our bed—with some creep. I just turned around and walked out. That was that. I provided her with funds to move out and get set up somewhere else. She tried, through the suit, to collect half of my property, which was pretty substantial. If she'd claimed I was the father of her child she might have got lucky. She never did. You know why?"

"No, Stan, why?"

"My lawyer was a smart guy," Stan said. "He had me take blood tests. I don't know the medical details but I understand there are ways to match blood samples. They could prove that you might be a child's father or that you couldn't possibly be. In judge's chambers we offered to face that match-up—my blood samples, the kid's blood samples. Nora wouldn't go for it. And so the judge ordered her lawyer not to even hint that I was her child's father or be in contempt. I believed at the time that Nora was sleeping around so much she had no idea who the father might be."

"Let's see. Nineteen sixty-eight, the kid under a year old," Eliot said. "That would make him about fifteen now. Just about the age of that thing under the canvas. Right?"

"What the hell are you getting at?" Stan asked, anger flaring.

"It can be pure coincidence," Eliot said. "But back in sixty-eight there were people who believed the rumor, or wanted to believe the rumor. We are a nation of people who like to hear dirt about the famous. Our anonymous phone caller just might be one of them. No? Do we know where Nora Sands is living now?"

"I haven't the faintest idea," Stan said. "I tell you, she's a bad dream I've forgotten until this moment."

"What the hell, boss, I know where Nora lives," Johnny Floyd burst in. "Right here in New York—in Greenwich Village. I've been in touch with her from time to time."

"Johnny!"

"She's been after you for more handouts. I was a sonofabitch if I'd let her mess up your life anymore. I took care of her from time to time, kept her out of your hair. The kid is about fifteen now."

"You recognized him and didn't say?" Hardy asked.

"I never saw the kid in my life," Johnny said. "But she talked about him when we met. That's why she needed dough, for the kid."

"How do we reach her?" Hardy asked.

Johnny reached in his pocket for his wallet. ''I have a phone number for her here.'' His cigarette was a stub between his thin lips. ''Don't be sore at me, boss. I just wanted to keep that mess out of your life again. You and Ellen and the kids didn't deserve that kind of stink in your life.''

And so it turned out that the murdered boy was known as Eddie Sands, that his mother was Nora Sands, and his father was take-your-pick.

THREE

I HAVE IMAGINED from time to time that I am a connoisseur of women. God knows they pass by me in the Beaumont in an endless parade, the grand ladies of American Society with a capital S, the beautiful foreign contingent, the women of kings, shahs, dictators, glamorous movie stars and Broadway actresses, American housewives who can be as exciting as all hell, professional call-girls whom we pretend not to see in our bars and corridors, and the young girls from everywhere, wide-eyed, rushing into whatever the future is. Women and girls! I have to tell you they make my teeth hurt. Not from chewing on them, but from standing back and letting them—most of them—pass.

I tell myself, as I approach my fortieth birthday, that my view of women has become more sophisticated than it was fifteen years ago. Now I tell myself that I am more concerned with personality, intellect, and wit than I am with simple physical beauty. But every now and then a woman comes along who is so loaded with sheer animal excitement that it doesn't matter if she can't add up to two.

Nora Sands took my breath away when I first saw her. I didn't get anywhere near her but it was like touching a live wire. She came running into the pool area, one of Hardy's cops behind her. She was down on her hands and knees, looking at the dead boy under the tarpaulin. From her came a cry of despair that ripped at my gut. No doubt, the dead boy was her kid.

She ignored everyone, including Stan Nelson, who stood a few yards away, the color drained from his face. There were things I knew about her as I watched, things I'd learned as we'd waited for her to arrive. She'd been eighteen when she'd shacked up with the young Stan Nelson in Hollywood, twenty when they separated, just over twenty-one when she'd sued him for a share of his property and lost. She'd been twenty-three when he married Ellen Davis, which made her thirty-five as she knelt beside her murdered son. At thirty-five she was in full bloom!

Johnny Floyd had done some talking while he waited. The year after the lawsuit Nora had posed for the center fold of the magazine *Private Lives,* stark naked—along with half a dozen other nude photographs in suggestive poses. That scurrilous magazine had not said in print that this luscious body had shared Stan Nelson's bed for two years, but a few hundred thousand people guessed it and slavered over the idea. I hadn't seen the pictures then, but I could imagine them. She had red hair, dark, violet eyes like Elizabeth Taylor's, and a figure that would have made Michelangelo breathe just a little harder.

"You can make an identification, Mrs. Sands?" Hardy asked, his voice quiet.

"*Miss* Sands," she said, not looking at him. Under other circumstances her husky voice would have been a magnet for interested males. She reached down to pick up the dead boy's hand and encountered some resistance. She looked up at Hardy, wide eyes wider.

"He's been dead quite a few hours—Miss Sands," the lieutenant said.

"Oh, my God!" she said.

"You can make a positive identification, Miss Sands?" Hardy hesitated. "His face—"

"Oh Jesus, you think I don't know my own son?" Nora Sands said. "I was about to show you. When he was a baby there was an accident. The little finger of his right hand got jammed in a door. They had to amputate it at the first joint. No fingertip or nail." She pointed down at the dead boy's stiffening right hand.

"So he is—"

"Eddie Sands, my son."

"Living at?"

"Forty-four Jane Street, in the Village."

"With you—Miss Sands?"

"Who else, for God sake!"

Hardy reached down and covered the mutilated face again. She grabbed the edge of the tarpaulin and yanked it back. She made a kind of moaning sound as she stared at the ugly wound.

"We have to move him, Miss Sands," Hardy said. "There has to be an autopsy."

"Cut him up?" she asked.

"A legal requirement," Hardy said.

"He could look better when they get through with him," Johnny Floyd said.

She turned her head, not to look at Johnny but at Stan Nelson, who was standing a little way off. "He came here to see you, Stan?" she asked.

His voice sounded far away, strained. "He came here to watch the telethon, Nora. I evidently signed an autograph for him but, of course, I had no idea who he was."

Nobody spoke for a minute and then Hardy picked up on it again. "You hadn't reported anywhere that he was missing—Miss Sands."

"I didn't know he was missing."

"He must have been here for hours when he was found," Hardy said. "You weren't surprised when he didn't come home last night?"

"I work at night," she said. "He was old enough to be left alone. There are people in the building he could ask for help if he needed it. I didn't get home till after nine o'clock this morning. He wasn't there, but I just supposed he'd gone out in the neighborhood somewhere to play with friends. He—he was on a stickball team. They often play on Saturday mornings. I went to bed. Your cop woke me up and told me."

"Where is it you work at night, Miss Sands?"

"The Private Lives Club. It's only a few blocks from where I live."

The publishers of *Private Lives Magazine* have a half a dozen or more of these nightclubs spread across the country. They don't rate very highly with churchgoers. They are designed to provide pleasure for single males, salesmen, delegates to conventions from out of town. They advertise, obliquely, that you could anticipate meeting a "Private Lives Girl" if you became a customer. A lot of these girls had posed for the famous nude photographs that were a feature of the magazine. If they hadn't they would, sooner or later. I've been told you could be provided with nude pictures before you picked out a companion for the evening. The law doesn't choose to recognize these places for what they really are.

"You'll pardon me for saying so, Miss Sands, but you strike me as being a little old to be working as a Private Lives Girl," Hardy said.

"I don't pardon you! My age is none of your business, Lieutenant. But—I'm the hostess at the club, not one of the girls," Nora Sands said.

"What time do you go to work?"

"Nine o'clock in the evening."

"And you work till nine o'clock in the morning? That's a long shift."

"I didn't say I was working till nine in the morning. I said I got home then."

"If your son had been home he wouldn't have been worried about you?"

"No. It wasn't unusual."

"It wasn't unusual for him to go out in the evening after you'd gone to work? Like here to the telethon?"

"It would have been unusual, without his leaving some kind of a note for me."

"He didn't leave a note last night?"

"No. So I didn't have any idea that he'd gone out till morning—for his stickball game."

"No note for that?"

"No. That was usual. He knew I'd know where he was."

"Breakfast?"

"Eddie is—was—a wonderfully neat boy. He got his own breakfast every morning, washed the dishes and silver and the frying pan if he cooked something—put them all away. I had no reason to think this morning wasn't perfectly normal when I got home."

"Do you know how we got on your track, Miss Sands?"

"The cop you sent said something about a phone call," Nora Sands said.

"An anonymous phone call," Hardy said. "Someone told us the dead boy was Stan Nelson's son. That led us to you."

"Oh boy, oh boy, oh boy!" she said. She leaned forward and covered her face with her hands for a moment. I was aware, for the first time, of a diamond ring about the size of a walnut.

Hardy waited for her to go on, but she didn't. The medical examiner's boys had come in with a stretcher and were waiting for instructions. Hardy gestured toward the tarpaulin, and the men began to lift the body onto the stretcher. Nora Sands grabbed at it, like a drowning person reached for a life raft.

"I'm sorry, Miss Sands," Hardy said.

The woman stood up. I guess I was the closest to her, which may explain the next thing that happened. She suddenly threw her arms around my shoulders and buried her face against my neck. Great, convulsive sobs shook her.

"Please, please, for God sake help me!" she whispered.

Chambrun spoke for the first time in all this interrogation. "There are better places to talk than this," he said. "What about my office, Walter?"

"I need some time here," Hardy said. "Your office would be fine, Pierre, but I don't want her leaving the hotel. I've only just started with Miss Sands." It seemed to bother him to use the word "Miss" for the mother of the dead boy.

THE MEDICAL TEAM CARRIED the body away. Stan Nelson, Johnny Floyd, and Butch Mancuso drifted off behind them, evidently permitted to use the freight elevator to go back to their suite on thirty-five. I was still being clung to by a sobbing Nora Sands. Chambrun gestured to me to take her away, down to his office. Hardy assigned one of his cops to go with us.

I instructed the elevator operator to take us directly to the second floor, and he did, ignoring the frantic lights on his light board. Betsy Ruysdale was waiting for us in her outer office. I should have known that Chambrun would have phoned down to forewarn her. She went with us into Chambrun's elegant office. I eased Nora Sands into one of the antique armchairs.

"Damn crybaby!" she said. "Is there a Kleenex in this joint?"

Ruysdale brought her one from the cabinet back of Chambrun's desk. "Would you like some coffee?" she asked Nora. "There's Turkish which I made for Mr.

Chambrun—which is ghastly. I have American out in my office."

Just the sound of Ruysdale's casual but friendly voice seemed to relax Nora. "What I'd really like is a drink, a good slug of bourbon. But you've got to be sure I don't take a second. I'm not to be trusted after one good one."

Ruysdale went over the Burmese cabinet and produced bourbon, ice in an old-fashioned glass. "Plain water or soda?" she asked.

"Very little plain water," Nora said. She drank the liquor almost straight down when Ruysdale handed it to her. A second short swig and she handed back the glass. "Just a touch more?"

"Sorry. Your orders," Ruysdale said, smiling at her. "If you'll excuse me, I've got things to do for the boss."

Nora leaned back in her chair and for a moment her shadowed eyelids closed down. Then they lifted and she was looking at me with those incredible violet eyes.

"Why me?" I asked her.

"Meaning?"

"Why did you ask me for help, grab onto me?"

"Funny. I don't even know your name," she said.

"Mark Haskell. I run public relations for the hotel."

"Who could I turn to?" she said. She gave out with a bitter little laugh. "Cops? Stan Nelson and his two goons must hate my guts. Your Mr. Chambrun looked like a judge on the bench. That left you, Mark."

"I hoped it was because I was irresistible, not just the best of a bad lot," I said.

"I've been making judgments about men ever since I was twelve years old," she said. "That's when I discovered my stepfather had more on his mind than playing doctor. I'm not very often wrong about them."

"You asked me up there in the club to help you, how?"

Her eyes narrowed and the warmth seemed to go out of them. "That wasn't an accident up there—what happened to Eddie. By the way, I get him back, don't I? I mean, for a decent funeral and all that?"

"Of course."

"How did he get there, Mark? How did he get up there in that pool?"

"We don't know that," I told her. "If everything happened the way it should—and we're told it did—there's no way he could get there. But he did."

"He didn't carry money," Nora said. "There are a thousand people in this hotel who would be better targets for a cheap mugging."

"He had two dollars and some change on him that wasn't taken," I said. "That and a green card on which Stan Nelson had signed his autograph."

"Can you imagine that? Stan signing something for him and not knowing who he was?"

"Did he know who Stan was?"

"How do you mean? Everybody knows who Stan is."

"That Stan had once been your guy, and that he just might be his father?"

"He knew that I used to know Stan. He didn't know any of the lurid details."

"You never told him?"

"It was coming up one of these days, but it hadn't—yet," she said almost bitterly.

"Why not? He was bound to hear about you and Stan sometime from somebody," I said.

"I wanted it to come from me, and somehow that 'right time' hadn't come," she said.

"Is Stan his father?"

She was silent for a moment, looking down at that huge diamond on her left-hand finger.

"If you were to ask one of the nice girls you know a question like that, she'd have the answer, wouldn't she? Will it shock you if I tell you I haven't the faintest idea who his father was?"

I have to admit it did shock me a little.

"Some people get hooked on liquor," she said. "Some on drugs. I've been hooked on sex all my life."

"You lived with Stan for two years. He supported you. You were committed to him, weren't you?"

"I gave him all he wanted," Nora said, a sharp edge on her voice. "It wasn't enough for me. Not nearly enough. And so, when he was away working, there were others. A lot of others."

"You could have claimed Stan was the boy's father and probably collected a lot of money from him," I said.

"I may be a bitch on wheels," she said, "but I wouldn't accuse my worst enemy of something I wasn't sure about. If you were to ask me right now, Mark, to go with you to wherever you live and make love to you I would."

My breathing felt a little thin!

"If I was pregnant after that I wouldn't accuse you," she said, "because there was someone else that night, and the night before that, and the night before that. That's how badly I'm hooked, Mark. I need it like water, or breakfast, or air!"

For once in my life I wanted to get away from that subject. I might ask, just for the excitement of it.

"Why would someone want to kill the boy?" I asked her. "Is there someone who wants to get even with you for something?"

"If there is he's going to wish he'd never been born when I find out who it is," she said. "The man on the telephone—he seems to have been trying to hurt Stan, wouldn't you say?"

It was true, we'd only guessed at her. The anonymous caller had never mentioned her.

"You had no idea your boy was going to go out last night to listen to Stan's telethon?"

"If this hadn't happened," she said, "and you asked me where Eddie might have gone last night, the last place on earth I'd have thought of would have been Stan's music. Eddie was born in the sixties; he grew up on the sounds of rock music and country music. He thought Stan's music—and Sinatra's, and Tony Bennett's, and Rosemary Clooney's—was old hat. He never listened to it at home on TV or radio. He collected records—all rock and country. I would never in the world guess he'd come here to hear Stan sing. He didn't collect autographs, trade them with other kids—a Stan Nelson for a Mick Jagger.''

''A personal interest in Stan—somebody slipped him the rumor that Stan might be his father, and he came to have a look?'' I suggested.

''Eddie and I were very close,'' she said, her husky voice lowered. ''If he'd heard a rumor like that he'd have asked me.''

''Did he—ask you about his father?''

''When he was old enough to realize that something was missing,'' she said. ''I wrote him a good tight scenario.'' Her smile had that bitter twist to it again. ''A whirlwind romance, I told him, just before his father had to go off to war—Vietnam. His father was dead, killed in action. That satisfied Eddie.''

''Didn't he wonder why his name was Sands—your name?''

''He had no reason not to think that was my married name.''

''Yet he came here and got Stan Nelson's autograph.''

''Did he?''

Both Nora and I turned sharply. Neither one of us had heard Chambrun come into the office. He walked past us and sat down at his desk.

''He had the autograph on him,'' I said.

Chambrun reached for one of his flat Egyptian cigarettes and got it going with his gold desk lighter. His eyes, not cordial, were narrowed against the smoke.

"You saw it," he said. "The boy's name wasn't on it. Stan doesn't put the names of the people he signs for when he gives an autograph. He told us that. He could have signed that pledge card for anyone and it can have been put in the boy's pocket later."

"Why?"

"Why any of it?" Chambrun said. "What was the boy doing here at the Beaumont if he wasn't interested in Stan or his music? I have to confess, Miss Sands, that I've been eavesdropping a little."

I glanced at the intercom on his desk. Ruysdale, ever efficient, had switched it on while she was in the office so that everything Nora and I said to each other could be heard out in her office. There was no First Amendment around here when Chambrun chose to invade your privacy. That didn't seem to bother Nora.

"I trust you enjoyed yourself," she said.

"There's been a murder in my hotel, Miss Sands. I'll do anything I can to get to the bottom of it. If your history, your habits, will help I'll use them."

"Help yourself," she said. "I want the answers just as badly as you do."

"Your work at the Private Lives Club here in the Village," he said. "This is well-organized, luxurious pornography all over the country. Hundreds of thousands of magazine readers looking at your nude photographs. Thousands of weak-minded males looking for free girls all across the country use the clubs."

"Free my foot," Nora said. "There's nothing free about anything Private Lives promotes anywhere."

"I used the word 'free' to apply to morals, not money," Chambrun said.

"Those nude pictures I posed for were fourteen years ago," Nora said. "Food isn't free, Mr. Chambrun. I had to eat!"

"And you've been working for Private Lives ever since?"

"Before that," she said. "I was a Private Lives Girl working in the Hollywood club when I met Stan. I was eighteen years old when he came there one night, looking for fun. He chose me, and afterwards he took me out of there. I lived with him for two years."

"But you still kept at your trade," Chambrun said.

"If you're suggesting I slept around for money, you're off your rocker, Chambrun."

"And when Stan walked out on you you went back to Private Lives?"

"For help," she said. "Zach Thompson thought Stan owed me. He got his own lawyer to handle my case. I guess he wasn't as good a lawyer as Zach thought."

"Zachary Thompson is the publisher of *Private Lives,* the operator of the clubs, the King of Porn?" Chambrun asked.

"He stood by me when I had no place else to turn," she said.

"And he's still standing by you?"

"When we lost the lawsuit against Stan he let me pose for the center fold of the magazine. There was a nice piece of change in that. I had a baby. I needed money wherever I could find it. He's found work for me, one way or another, ever since."

"He's your lover?"

She laughed. "Zach doesn't stay put long enough for anyone to think of his as 'theirs.' He has thousands of beautiful girls to choose from, anytime, day or night." She nodded towards the intercom. "I hope your secretary isn't sitting out there blushing."

"She just might be," Chambrun said. "Ruysdale has different ideas about the man-woman relationship than you do, Miss Sands."

"Maybe she doesn't know what she's missing," Nora said. She could really play it tough.

Chambrun crushed out his cigarette in the ashtray on his desk as though he was angry at it. "Would Eddie have talked to any friends before he set out for the Beaumont last night? Kids he was close to, his stickball friends?"

"I suppose he might have."

"Give me some names," Chambrun said, pulling a legal pad toward him and picking up a ball-point pen.

"I don't intend to involve kids in this mess," Nora said.

"Somebody put a magnum-sized gun to that boy's face and blew a hole in him," Chambrun said. "You want that someone to go free?"

"No!"

"So, names, please!"

The phone light blinked on Chambrun's desk. He picked it up, and Betsy Ruysdale's voice came through the intercom. "There's a man named Zachary Thompson and a lawyer named Wallach here to see Miss Sands," she said.

Chambrun drew a deep breath. "Bring them in. By the way, Ruysdale, *were* you blushing?"

"I think I'll skip lunch," she said.

Zachary Thompson doesn't have the familiar face of a movie star, but hundreds of thousands of people would know him by sight. His picture appears on the masthead of his magazine *Private Lives,* on the advertisements of his Private Lives clubs, and all too frequently in the press and on television news shows. In the last year Greta Jansen, the film star, has been suing Thompson for what she claimed were libelous statements in the magazine, plus some pretty steamy photographs of her in a nude scene in a foreign film. It was all grist to the Thompson mill, gave him endless exposure, plus in the end the courts ruled in his favor. The actress had made that nude scene for public distribution—in the film, of course—and she had made a spectacle of herself under the influence of drugs in a famous Hollywood restaurant. *Private Lives* had reported on public facts, the court ruled, and not invaded the lady's privacy. Drinks were free in all the Private Lives clubs across the country the night the verdict came in.

Zach Thompson has to be at least fifty years old. He's been running what Chambrun calls his "porno empire" for twenty-five years. As he walked into

Chambrun's office he looked like a slightly overage hippie, with his long hair, his Fu Manchu mustache and pointed beard, wearing blue jeans, a garish orange sports shirt, a chamois vest with no jacket over it. He walked straight to Nora, ignoring Chambrun and me, and took the woman in his arms.

"Now, now, baby, just take it easy," he said. "Papa's here."

She accepted his embrace, snuggling her face against his beard. He looked over her head at Chambrun. "You're Pierre Chambrun?"

"You weren't admitted into the men's room," Chambrun said.

"So, we're going to play hard ball, are we?" Thompson said. "This is Lou Wallach, my lawyer."

Wallach looked a little more civilized to me than his client. A businessman's haircut, a pale gray tropical worsted summer suit, a white shirt with a tie with regimental stripes. Probably a Brooks Brothers customer, I thought.

"I understand the police are holding Nora, not allowing her to leave the hotel," Thompson said. "On what charges?"

"Somebody killed Eddie," Nora said in a husky whisper.

"Do they say you did it, Baby?"

"It's awful, Zach. His whole face was blown away."

"Do they say you did it?"

"They don't say anything yet. They don't know anything yet, Zach."

"Then we'll just hightail it out of here," Thompson said. "You got any objection to make, Chambrun?"

"The air might be a little fresher," Chambrun said.

Thompson put the girl aside, gently, and took a step toward Chambrun's desk. "You want to make cheap wisecracks I'm liable to wash out your mouth with soap, Dad," he said.

"I just wanted to be sure I spoke a language you'd understand," Chambrun said.

Thompson took another quick step toward the desk.

"Cool it, Zach," the lawyer said. His voice was quiet, level. "Is Miss Sands being detained here, Mr. Chambrun?"

"It isn't quite that way, Lou," Nora said, before Chambrun could answer. "It was so awful up there in the Health Club where it happened. Mr. Chambrun kindly offered to let me wait here till the cop in charge could ask me questions about Eddie."

"What kind of questions?" Thompson asked.

"Who blew his brains out and why," Chambrun said.

"They don't know who or why?" Thompson asked.

"They didn't even know who Eddie was, when they found him," Nora said. "He wasn't carrying anything on him that would identify him."

"How did they get to you?" Lou Wallach asked.

"An anonymous phone call," Nora said. "A man phoned the police and told them Eddie was Stan Nelson's son. Someone knew Stan and I had once been close. They asked me to try to identify Eddie, and of course, I could."

"Stan Nelson's here in the hotel, isn't he?" Thompson asked.

"Yes, he is," Nora said. "He did his cancer telethon here last night."

"Sonofabitch!" Thompson said. "I hope to God they haven't let him take off. Mr. Big Shot!"

"You brought a suit against Nelson some years ago, didn't you, Wallach?" Chambrun asked.

"I wasn't Zach's lawyer in those days," Wallach said.

"Nora brought the suit," Thompson said. "I supplied the lawyer. A square-headed judge ruled against her. She ought to be living in clover off Mr. Big Shot instead of working for me. I stand by my people, which is more than can be said for Nelson."

"I know you don't have to answer questions from me, Mr. Chambrun," Wallach said. "But just what did happen here in your hotel?"

Chambrun hesitated for a moment, and then reached for another cigarette. He lighted it and leaned back in his chair. "I don't mind telling you what I know, Mr. Wallach," he said, "because it isn't really anything. The day manager of the Health Club came to work a little before nine. He started to check out the place before he opened it up for the public and found Eddie Sands, floating in the pool, dead of a gunshot wound in the face that exited out the back of his head. The police were called. As Miss Sands has told you, he had no identification on him."

"Stan had signed an autograph for him," Nora said. "He must have come here for the telethon."

"There was an autograph on a pledge card," Chambrun said. "Nelson doesn't ask for names of people for whom he signs an autograph, so the card didn't help identify the boy."

"Nelson signed an autograph for him?" Thompson exploded. "He must have known who he was!"

"He didn't. Hundreds of kids crowding around him. They hand him a card, he signed. That was that."

"He knew, for Christ sake!"

"He says he never saw the boy—ever."

"My foot! He had to be curious. He had to want to take a look at him sometime over the years. He knew he could be the boy's father!"

"Miss Sands says she doesn't know."

"She couldn't prove it, but she knows it!"

"No, Zach!" Nora said.

"She's let him off the hook all these years because she is too damned decent!" Thompson said. "Maybe Eddie threatened to tell the world if Nelson didn't come through. Eddie was dreaming of college—stuff like that. He had a right to hang it on Nelson! He's Nelson's kid!"

"No, Zach!" Nora cried.

"You want facts, Mr. Wallach?" Chambrun asked.

"Please," Wallach said.

"There is no gun anywhere in the Health Club. There is no indication where the actual shooting took place. The boy obviously bled profusely—pints and pints. If he was shot in the water there's no way to prove it out. The water circulates in the pool and if the bleeding took place there only a few streaks of blood are left. There is no sign of the bullet, which obviously exited from the back of the boy's head. Those are facts, Mr. Wallach—or you might say those are facts we don't have."

"He could have been shot somewhere else and taken to the pool later," Wallach suggested.

"The night shift gets rid of the customers at ten P.M.," Chambrun said. "It takes about an hour or more for the crew to clean up, the keys deposited in the key safe in the main lobby office. All that happened. No body."

"So he was taken in later," Thompson said impatiently.

"Everything properly locked, no doors forced," Chambrun said.

"What are you, for God sake, trying to do? Tell us it didn't happen?"

"I'm telling you, Thompson, that there is no way it could have happened—but it did."

Thompson gave me a sardonic smile. "So Buster here can write another one of his crime stories. The murder that didn't happen, but it did."

Wallach seemed not to be listening to the byplay. "The boy was obviously in the hotel during the evening, alive and well. The Nelson autograph proves that."

"Does it?" Chambrun asked, knocking the ash from his cigarette.

"Well of course it does!" Thompson said.

"Hundreds and hundreds of people got autographs from Nelson during the twenty-four hours of the telethon," Chambrun said. "They're all as alike as peas in a pod. No individual names on them. That autograph can have been signed for someone else and planted on the boy later. He could have been killed in his own apartment, the autograph planted on him, the body brought here."

"You some kind of a stand-up comic?" Thompson said. "A million people circulating in the lobby while the telethon was in progress. You can carry a dead man through that crowd? If I know how you run things, the service areas were pretty well policed by your security people during that time. You wouldn't want strange geeks going up and down the back ways in your hotel. You carry a dead man that way? He was murdered in your plush whorehouse, Chambrun, and you know it! Bad publicity, but you can't duck it."

"It's a possibility," Chambrun admitted, "but tell me how the body was gotten into the pool after the Health Club was closed and locked."

"That's your problem, not mine," Thompson said. "But I can make a guess where the murder happened, and I'll bet you haven't even bothered to look."

"I'm listening," Chambrun said.

"The kid came here to put the heat on his old man, Stan Nelson," Thompson said. "Nelson, I suppose, has a suite here. No? The kid had something he could make stick, and that Warner Brothers' gangster-type who acts as a bodyguard for Nelson shot him. He had the rest of the night to get the body down to the Health Club."

Chambrun turned his cold eyes to Nora. "When was the last time you saw your boy alive, Miss Sands?"

She hesitated a moment. "Breakfast yesterday morning, Friday morning," she said. "I was just coming from—from work, and he was taking off for school."

"He didn't come home before you went to work on Friday night? Didn't come home for supper?"

"I told you, he's stickball crazy," Nora said. "On Fridays, when he doesn't have homework to do, they play after school—till the daylight gives out. That's around eight-thirty, daylight time, these days. If he stops for a hamburger, or just to chew the rag with his friends, he wouldn't get home before I go to work. It's nothing unusual on Friday nights."

Chambrun looked back at Thompson. "The telethon started the preceding midnight," he said. "It had been going on a little over eight hours when Miss Sands last saw her son. Nelson was in the ballroom all that time and for sixteen hours after that. So was Mancuso, the bodyguard. So was Floyd, the other man sharing the suite with Nelson. They had their own dressing room and john down there. They never left the ballroom area."

"So it happened after the telethon was over. The kid waited, went up to Nelson's suite, and got it between the eyes! They've had plenty of time to clean up any mess, get rid of the missing bullet, clean Mancuso's gun so it won't seem to have been fired recently. You wait long enough and they'll all be back in California, safe and sound.''

It was farfetched, but it couldn't be ignored. In addition to Zach Thompson and Wallach there was a Mr. Anonymous, pushing us in Stan Nelson's direction. We didn't know it, but while we were talking in Chambrun's office, Lieutenant Hardy had received another call from our anonymous informant.

"Don't let Stan Nelson go till he tells you when and where he talked with his son."

Our switchboard had been alerted to try to trace the call the next time Mr. Anonymous got in touch. Hardy tried to keep him talking to give them a chance, but he spoke just the one sentence and hung up before there was any time for a trace.

Hardy was not a man to avoid going down any side street, no matter how unlikely. So it was that after listening to Thompson's nonsense—nonsense was my word for it—Chambrun, Hardy, and I went up to the thirty-fifth floor, with a plain-clothes cop in tow.

It was obvious when we reached 35C that Stan and his two aides were preparing to leave. Bags had been packed and were standing near the front door. Stan was sitting in a chair by the windows overlooking Central Park, sipping coffee resting on a tray that had obviously been brought to him by room service. Butch Mancuso was across the room, reading the sports pages of the *Daily News*.

"I was beginning to wonder if you were going to get here in time, Lieutenant," Stan said. "Johnny Floyd's trying to settle our bill down in the lobby."

"Time for what?" Hardy asked.

"We have flight reservations for Vegas at five o'clock," Stan said. "I'm supposed to open out there tomorrow night. The Oasis."

"We've had another call from our anonymous friend," Hardy said. "Don't let Stan Nelson go till he tells you when and where he talked with his son."

"Oh for God sake, who is this freak who keeps trying to involve me?" Stan asked.

"I wish we knew," Hardy said. "No luck trying to trace his calls."

"Shall I say it all once more for you, Lieutenant?" Stan sounded like a man whose patience was running out, not a tense or a nervous man. "I have never to my knowledge laid eyes on Nora's son since the day he was born."

"But you knew he existed? You knew that fourteen years ago when she sued you for a property settlement."

"Yes."

"You read the newspapers at the time, didn't you? You knew there was gossip that you might be the child's father?"

"Of course I knew," Stan said. "I even thought I might be. Nora and I had lived together for two years."

"You weren't interested enough to try to see him?"

Stan put down his coffee cup hard in its saucer. "It came up, in a pretrial hearing," he said. "I offered to take whatever the tests are that might prove or disprove my involvement. Nora's lawyer turned down the offer. Presumably she knew I wasn't the father. I think she and her lawyer preferred to have the rumor stay alive than to have evidence that I was not involved. Can you understand? I never wanted to see the boy. He was the result of her messing around with other men when I thought she was mine. I didn't want to see him. I didn't want to see her. I never have seen him, and I haven't seen her since the trial until this morning, down there by the pool. I don't want to see her again now, unless I have to."

"You know Zach Thompson?" Hardy asked.

"That bastard! Yes, I know him. Nora was working for him when I first met her."

"At this Hollywood club?"

"Yes."

"You were a customer. She was a girl you picked out, however those choices were made?"

Stan's mouth turned down at the corners in an expression of distaste. "I don't like to remember how I was living in those days," he said. "That was seventeen years ago. I was twenty-five. Scrambling to make a living in a town full of wolves. I hadn't made it then. Johnny Floyd took me to that Private Lives Club. Just something to do. They showed you pictures of girls, dressed and undressed. You made your choice. The girl I chose was Nora. I—I fell in love with her."

"You persuaded her to quit her job and settle in with you?"

"Yes. I struck it big just about then, in a film. I suddenly had the money to keep a woman in luxury."

"I'd like to ask a question if I may, Walter," Chambrun said.

"Go," Hardy said.

"How much damage can it do your career, Nelson—this reviving of the rumor that Eddie Sands was your son?"

"This is not 1930," Stan said. "The big studios guarded the reputations of their stars in those days like it was gold in Fort Knox. You didn't hear any scandal about a Joan Crawford until she was dead! It's different today. The woods are full of kids out there whose parents aren't married. The Census Bureau even has a name for them—POSSLQs. People of Opposite Sex Sharing Living Quarters. Today a fifteen-year-old-kid from a live-together wouldn't raise a ripple. But a murder is something else!"

"Our anonymous friend isn't just calling the police, you know," Chambrun said. "He's throwing his curveball to the press, radio, TV. It sets them all free to report his call, spread the gossip, without claiming it's a fact."

"The more they spread it the more customers they'll turn away at the Oasis in Vegas tomorrow night," Butch Mancuso said. "People thrive on dirt these days."

"So you're not disturbed by the talk?" Hardy asked Stan.

"I'm disturbed by the murder," Stan said. "I'm disturbed that some freak is trying to point at me. I'm disturbed for Nora, whatever our past may be. It's her son, her kid. I'm disturbed that some crazy is floating around with a gun who may have another target in mind. This anonymous creep may be that killer. That disturbs me."

"Would it disturb you to know that it's been suggested that the boy came up here to this suite after the telethon was over, accused you of something, threatened you with something, and that he was shot by Mancuso, or Johnny Floyd—or you, Nelson?"

Stan just stared at Hardy, apparently not believing what he heard.

"What bullshit!" Mancuso exploded.

"You carry a gun, Mancuso?" Hardy said.

Mancuso flipped open his jacket. "Sure I do," he said. "And I've got a license to carry it."

"In my city?"

"Your city, any city we go to. I got a dozen licenses."

"Mind if I look at it?"

Mancuso yanked the gun out of its holster and handed it to Hardy. It looked like a .38 police special, not big enough to blow the kind of hole we'd seen in Eddie Sands' face. Hardy sniffed at the barrel of the gun, checking its loading.

"I haven't had to use it to protect Stan for a long time," Mancuso said. "I practice with it to keep my hand in."

"Let me see your license for New York City," Hardy said.

Mancuso took a wallet from an inner pocket, fumbled around in it and came up with what Hardy wanted. After a moment Hardy handed back the gun.

"At least this one is legal," he said.

"What do you mean 'this one'?"

"You could have another gun, not licensed," Hardy said. "It could be in your luggage, or you can have gotten rid of it after you used it."

"I think that's going just a little too far, Lieutenant," Stan said. "No one came up here after the telethon. That is, no one came in here. There were people out in the hall, trying to get a last-minute autograph, or grab off a handkerchief or a piece of my clothing. Butch and Johnny kept them out. That's par for the course."

The front door to the suite opened and Johnny Floyd came in. He was a man burning with anger. When he saw Chambrun he waggled a finger at him.

"Why aren't you downstairs managing this lousy fleabag of yours, Chambrun? There's a million reporters down there and that jerk, Zach Thompson, holding court! He's told everybody this side of China that the dead boy is probably Stan's kid. I had to fight my way to the desk to get a bill and pay it!"

Butch Mancuso started for the door, but Sergeant Lawson, Hardy's man, blocked the way.

"You want to have big trouble, Buster, just keep standing there," Mancuso said.

"Keep it down, Butch," Stan Nelson said.

"I just want to hear that Thompson smear you once, Stan!" Mancuso said. "After that they can run a picture of what's left of him in his stinking magazine."

"Just take it easy," Stan said. He turned to Hardy. "You haven't asked yet, Lieutenant, but I suggest you came up here to search the suite and our belongings."

"He better keep his sticky fingers off my stuff!" Mancuso said.

"Let's get it over with, Butch. We have a plane to catch," Stan said.

The search began, slow and methodical. Sergeant Lawson went down the corridor to the bedrooms. Hardy had Stan, Johnny Floyd, and Mancuso each open their bags and stand by as he went through the contents.

Chambrun stood by, silent, frowning. When Stan Nelson's personal belongings had been checked out, the bags repacked and closed up, he beckoned to the singer and they stood together over by the windows. I maneuvered myself close enough to listen.

"Hardy is a very thorough man," Chambrun said. "You did the right thing turning him loose. He could have kept you tied up forever while he got a court order, search warrants. If there's anything to hide, it will be over quickly this way."

"Did Nora have anything to offer? She was down in your office, wasn't she?"

"Nothing that took us anywhere," Chambrun said. "Then Zach Thompson appeared with his lawyer and that was that."

"It was Thompson who suggested the boy came up here—that one of us killed him?"

"Wild talk," Chambrun said.

"For fifteen years that sonofabitch has been nipping at my heels," Stan said. A little nerve twitched high up on his cheek. "The whole damned world, thanks to him at the time, knew what happened between me and Nora. The film critic in his stinking magazine always blasts my performance in a film. His music critic pans my records."

"And yet you are a very, very rich man," Chambrun said.

There was a sardonic twist to Stan's smile. "I've come to think that praise for me in *Private Lives* would be bad luck. I don't think Thompson's ever forgiven me for defeating Nora's property suit against me. I suspect he looked forward to taking a slice of the proceeds for the rest of time if she'd won."

"What would have been a lot of money?"

Stan gave Chambrun the kind of weary smile that goes with answering a question for the umpteenth time. "Would you believe, Mr. Chambrun, that I can't estimate how much? You must have wondered, earlier down in the Health Club, how it was that Johnny Floyd knew where Nora was living, and that he'd apparently taken care of her financial needs to keep me from being worried. He took care of her with *my* money, Mr. Chambrun. Would you believe that a street kid, who started life playing piano in a local house of ill repute, turned out to be a financial wizard? I am an innocent musician who hears the melody of a tune, the romance or humor of a lyric and not much else. Johnny Floyd played for me in the beginning, and he also handled my money. It used to be fifty bucks a night for both of us at the start. It's more than a hundred times that now. Johnny took care of the dough, then and now, and he's invested in oil, in real estate. It's multiplied and multiplied, thanks to Johnny. If Nora had won her suit against me and been awarded a percentage of my income for the rest of my life, she would have been a very rich woman."

"Johnny has access to your funds so he could take care of her when she was in trouble?" Chambrun asked.

"Yes."

"You trust him with what is obviously a substantial fortune?"

Stan smiled across the room at his bald-headed friend. "With my life," he said. "A friend is a friend is a friend is a friend. That's Johnny."

Chambrun's voice was cold. "Would he kill the boy if he thought Eddie was threatening you with harm?"

Stan actually laughed. "Johnny has a temper," he said, "but he isn't, for Christ sake, a killer. And what harm could the boy have threatened?"

Lieutenant Hardy came across the room to join us.

"In the sense of any kind of physical evidence," the detective said, "this suite and your luggage appear to be clean, Mr. Nelson."

"I wasn't waiting in suspense, Lieutenant," Stan said.

"I'd like very much not to have to take legal steps to prevent you from catching that five o'clock flight to Vegas," Hardy said. "But I'd like very much for you to stay put for a while—here, in the hotel."

Stan frowned. "I have a contractual obligation to appear in Vegas tomorrow night," he said.

"The people at the Oasis would surely understand why you might have to stay over," Hardy said. "They watch TV, listen to radio, read the newspapers."

"They might understand, Lieutenant," Stan said. "But I don't. Why do you want me to stay on? I may or may not have signed an autograph for the dead boy. That's my total involvement."

"You are the target of our anonymous phone caller," Hardy said. "We are set up here at the Beaumont to trace his next call, when and if it comes. If we can pick him up and you can identify him we may be on the way to solving a homicide."

Johnny Floyd had joined us. "We're already checked out, bill paid, taxi ordered," he said. He always seemed angry about everything, cigarette bobbing up and down between his lips.

"Now that this story has broken the whole bloody world is trying to get at me," Stan said. "I dare you to take a look down in the lobby."

"I know," Hardy said. "The word's out that you're leaving. So you stay put. It could only be a few hours, a day or two at most."

"I think I can give you privacy, Nelson," Chambrun said. "There are three penthouses on the roof. I live in one, an old lady who has been a tenant for more than thirty years has the second. The third is kept available for important diplomats coming to the United Nations. That one happens to be available at the moment.''

''You don't have to make yourself bait for some crazy, Stan,'' Johnny Floyd said. ''Let's get out of here!''

''Only one elevator goes to the roof,'' Chambrun said. ''The operator won't take anyone up there who hasn't been okayed by me, Mrs. Haven, or whoever is in number three. No press, no autograph hounds, no one you don't authorize. We can keep you safer than you would be anywhere else. Until this anonymous troublemaker is out of the way I don't think you could do better, Nelson.''

''Let 'em clean up their own mess!'' Johnny Floyd urged.

Stan was silent for a moment. ''We'll stay—for a while, at least,'' he said.

STAN NELSON and Johnny Floyd were right about the lobby down on the main floor. It was a madhouse. Those of us who, I suppose you could say, had been on the ''inside'' since Carl Hulman had found a dead boy in the Health Club pool had not been really aware of the ghoulish excitement caused by TV and radio in the first two or three hours. That was all thanks to our anonymous phone caller and his hints about Stan Nelson.

The Beaumont had been invaded by an army of people who had probably never been inside its doors before, three quarters of them young female shriekers. Stan would have to appear sooner or later, and they would scream at him, cheer and jeer at him, and unless he was carefully protected, tear off his clothes. In addition to the shriekers and the rubberneckers there were the press, TV, and radio people. It was their job to be there, to get some kind of statement from Hardy, from Stan himself, and in a minor league way from me, representing the hotel. I could, they supposed, tell them where Stan was and they could charge after him like a runaway army.

I wasn't telling, of course. While I found myself in the center of a whirlpool of screeching fans and demanding reporters, Stan Nelson and Johnny Floyd and Butch Mancuso were being quietly escorted up to the penthouse on the roof by Chambrun and Jerry Dodd. Once they were safely there we could begin to deal with the swarm of unwanted ghouls who had taken over our world.

I had a standard answer to the questions with which I was being smothered. "Stan is still being interrogated by the police."

"Is the dead boy Stan's son?"

"Do the police think Stan killed him?"

"Did Stan identify the boy for them?"

And then there was a question I couldn't ignore. It came from my friend Eliot Stevens of International, who had managed to maneuver himself next to me in the center of the mob.

"So you've slipped him out of the hotel while we wait here yammering?" he asked.

"'For Your Eyes Only,'" I said, approximating the title of the latest James Bond movie. "When he says 'yes,' Eliot, you'll be the first to hear it. He's still in the hotel but out of reach."

"Chambrun's penthouse?" he asked.

"Close," I said.

"Okay, chum. But just remember I'll hang the Beaumont out to dry if you try to bypass me on this."

"Just come up with an idea how to get rid of all these creeps without turning a fire hose on them and Chambrun may give you his right arm."

"You'd be surprised how easy it is," he said. He moved away and stood up on one of the lobby chairs, waving his arms for silence. When he could be heard he identified himself. "I'm Eliot Stevens of International," he shouted at them. "I've just been informed by the hotel that Stan Nelson has been taken down to police headquarters on Centre Street. If you hope to see him that's the place to go and wait."

There were howls of disappointment, and then people began to jostle themselves out onto the street, like a receding tidal wave. Eliot gave me a wry smile.

"So, business as usual, provided you play ball, Buster," he said.

Instantly a clean-up crew was in action picking up candy wrappers, empty cigarette packs, crumpled papers, and other garbage. In fifteen minutes the Beaumont lobby would be its usual elegant self. I saw Mr. Atwater, the head desk clerk, waving at me. I went over to him.

Andy Atwater is a kind of professional greeter for new guests who are just signing in. He has a professional smile and professional cheerfulness. At this moment he looked like he'd eaten something that disagreed with him, his face white, mouth tight and unsmiling. I supposed the invasion of the shriekers had unsettled him.

"They won't be back soon, Andy," I told him.

"Mr. Chambrun wants you down on the truck-loading platform in the basement," Atwater said. "They found Tony Camargo down there, stuffed in a laundry hamper, beaten to death they say. What the hell's going on around here, Mr. Haskell?"

PART TWO

ONE

IT WAS JUST a little while ago—a few hours actually—that Tony Camargo, the bright-eyed young Italian night manager of the Health Club, had stood next to me describing his nightly closing procedure to Lieutenant Hardy. It was his testimony that had set up what Chambrun had called a "classic locked-room mystery"—how could Eddie Sands' body have been deposited in the pool when there was no way to get it there?

Believe it though, I didn't imagine for an instant as I took the rear service elevator down to the loading platform that there was any connection between the shooting of Eddie Sands and some kind of mugging attack on Tony Camargo. I should have had my head examined.

There is a substreet-level parking garage under the Beaumont. There is also a separate service ramp for trucks bringing in food supplies, liquor, and other daily needs along with space for other trucks that cart away trash, laundry that goes to a big hotel service, equipment that our maintenance crew can't repair and needs to go back to the manufacturer for rebuilding. One of the regular routines is the mid-afternoon pickup by the laundry service. Soiled sheets, pillowcases, towels, and other linens from the restaurants and bars are stuffed in large hampers by the maid service and other crews and taken down to the loading platform. The routine hadn't varied on this day. The laundry service brought back the hampers from the day before, filled now with washed and ironed linens, and prepared to take away the soiled accumulation. The trucking boys had noticed that one of the take-away hampers seemed unusually heavy. They opened the wicker lid to the hamper and saw nothing but used sheets and towels. As they were closing the lid one of the men glanced down and saw that they'd moved the hamper away from a pool of blood that it had covered in its original position. Taking out the top layer of soiled laundry they discovered the beaten and mangled body of a man.

Ironically, Manhattan Homicide was already installed in the Beaumont. There was no problem this time about identifying the body. Lieutenant Hardy had interrogated Tony Camargo earlier in the day. Chambrun had been summoned down from the penthouse area where he'd been settling in Stan Nelson and his two companions. He was in a cold fury when I joined the crowd of cops and stunned-looking employees on the loading platform. The murder of Eddie Sands had been an impersonal kind of problem-puzzle to him. Tony Camargo was *his* boy, one of *his* people.

"Extraordinary coincidence," I heard Sergeant Lawson, Hardy's man, say.

"Coincidence my foot!" Chambrun said. He glared at Hardy who gave him a questioning look. "Simple answer is always there for a locked-room puzzle, you said, Walter. Tony was going to remember, sooner or later, something that would explain how the Sands boy got into the pool upstairs. Somebody made sure he'd never get to remember and tell us."

If God had spoken I couldn't have been surer that He was right. I could see that Hardy had bought it, too.

On the wall at the back of the loading platform there was a collection of tools for emergency use—a hammer, a screwdriver, a hatchet. I don't remember all the items except for the iron wrecking bar. It was no longer in its place. It had been discarded down onto the roadway of the ramp and was lying under the laundry truck, covered with blood. No doubt it was the weapon used to crush Tony's head like an over-ripe melon. On the wall where the tools hung there were spatters of blood for a distance of about four feet, and on the floorboards of the platform in that area. No doubt about where the attack had taken place.

"Man beaten to death and no one sees or hears anything," Hardy muttered, almost to himself.

"Tony never made a sound after the first blow was struck," Chambrun said. "The medical examiner will tell you that, I'm sure."

"What was he doing down here?" Sergeant Lawson asked.

"That's simple enough," Jerry Dodd, our security chief, told him. "He was home, off duty, when we called him to ask him to come down here to talk to

Lieutenant Hardy about the trouble upstairs. He lives in the Bronx. He drove down in an old Toyota he owns, parked it in the garage like every day. He was on the way to get his car and go out when this happened.''

"Anyone could drive in off the street and wait for him down here," Sergeant Lawson said.

"We don't run a cheap flophouse here, Sergeant," Jerry said. "You don't just 'drive in' the garage. If you're a guest in the hotel, or you're coming here for a meal, or to visit someone, you go to the front entrance, the doorman gives you a ticket for your car, one of our parking attendants puts it down here for you. When you leave, you give your ticket to the doorman and he sends for your car. People don't wander around down here who don't belong here."

"You're saying someone who does belong down here killed him?" Lawson said.

"I'm just saying this area wasn't crawling with strangers," Jerry said. "When you've had a chance to talk to the parking attendants and the garage people you may come up with someone who saw a stranger down here."

"Trucks, like this laundry vehicle, come and go," Hardy said.

"It's not a thruway," Jerry said. "At the top of the ramp there's a gate. There's a man operating it. He doesn't open the gate till he knows you're supposed to be here."

"The whole hotel has been crowded with people who aren't normally here," Hardy said. "Stan Nelson's twenty-four-hour telethon, then again this morning and early afternoon after the news broke about Eddie Sands up in the pool. Normal security must break down in times like that, because everybody is a stranger to your security people, Dodd. Thousands of them in the space of a day and a half."

"Strangers weren't holding a meeting down here," Jerry said.

Scotty McPherson, the daytime engineer on duty, had the closest thing to a helpful story. He's a big, lumbering man who can handle a pinpoint electrical connection with fingers as agile as a cardsharp's.

"Tony stopped by my office—couldn't have been ten minutes before it happened," Scotty told us.

"Where is your office?" Hardy asked.

"Just down the corridor there. I call it an office, but it's really a room where I have all the instrument panels in front of me. Tony and I are old friends. He's worked in the hotel for some ten years, I guess. Ever since he got the Health Club job—what is it, five, six years—he'd come to work about four-thirty, park his car, and walk past my place on his way to the service elevator. He'd stick his head in the door and say 'hello.' Always laughing and kidding. He had a collection of Polish jokes as long as your arm."

"No Scotch jokes?" Hardy asked him, deadpan.

"He knew better," McPherson said. "I don't come on till noon, so I didn't see him when he arrived this morning. Not the usual time for him. When you guys got through with him in the Health Club he came by

my place. I'd had the word about the trouble upstairs, and naturally we talked about it."

"What did he tell you?"

"Only that everything had been shipshape when he
left last midnight. Nobody in the pool, no way anyone could hide up there or get in after he'd gone, but
somebody had, did."

"Did he suggest how?"

"He just kept saying there was no way, and yet it
had happened," McPherson said.

"You say that was about ten minutes before he was
attacked, Scotty," Chambrun interrupted. "How do
you arrive at that kind of timing?"

"Figuring backwards," Scotty said. "This laundry
truck driver came screaming down the hall that there
was a dead man in one of the laundry hampers.
There's an electric clock on the wall in my place. I
looked at it then and it was just three-thirty-five. The
laundry truck usually arrives about three-thirty. They
were on schedule. It seemed like Tony had only just
left me. But there had to be time for someone to slug
him, jam his body in that laundry hamper, and take
off before the truck pulled in. It must have happened
as soon as he walked from my place down the corridor to here."

"And you didn't hear anything? Didn't hear Camargo call for help?" Hardy asked.

"Just listen for a minute, Lieutenant," Scotty said.

No one spoke for a moment. You could hear the
noise of the machinery that runs the elevators, the
sound of car motors in the garage. A metallic voice

came over a loud-speaker. "Car number one eighty-two at the front entrance, please." The doorman had a customer for the parking attendants.

"You can't whisper down here, Lieutenant," Scotty said. "If I'd heard somebody shout I wouldn't have paid any attention to it, most likely. I'd have thought it was one of the parking boys shouting something at one of the others."

"You're sure Tony didn't suggest he had any theory about what happened in the Health Club, Scotty?" Chambrun asked again.

"Just that it couldn't have happened but it did," Scotty said. "He said he was going out to see a guy before he had to check back in for his shift."

"What guy?"

Scotty shrugged. "He just said he was going to see a guy."

"He didn't suggest this 'guy' might have answers about what happened in the Health Club?"

"He didn't say so. He didn't act like it," Scotty said.

"Damn," Chambrun said.

A slim, blond young man came down the corridor onto the loading platform. He had a blond mustache and rather long sideburns. His blue eyes were red as though he'd been crying.

"Somebody just phone me at home about what happened, Mr. Chambrun," he said. "My God, how awful!"

He was Jimmy Heath, Tony Camargo's assistant, who had helped Tony close up the night before.

We'd had, you might say, a death in the family.

THE BEAUMONT DOESN'T operate on a stool-pigeon
system, though an outsider might have thought so. It
was like a vast machine made up of meshing cog-
wheels. Be a little off-timing on one operation and you
could start the whole machinery to bumping and
thumping. "For want of a nail the shoe was lost, for
want of a shoe the horse was lost—" The first time
something went out of kilter there were inquiries as to
why and whatever was wrong was corrected. If it went
wrong a second time you could expect a thunderbolt
to be dropped from heaven, which in the Beaumont
means Chambrun's office.

In the space of twenty-four hours the machinery had
malfunctioned twice, routines had fouled up twice,
and it had cost two lives. Hardy could go on the medical examiner's report on a gunshot and beating
wounds, on what his fingerprint experts and photographers could produce at the two murder scenes, on
the hope of tracking down the anonymous phone
caller who obviously knew more than he had any
business knowing, the police lab report on dirt and fi-
bers found on Eddie Sands' body that might provide
a clue as to where the boy had been killed.

Chambrun, who played the game by intuition and
hunch, was faced in another direction. Something had
fouled up in the smooth functioning of his world.
Tony Camargo had missed something that would explain how Eddie Sands' body got into the pool, and
before he could remember it someone who had no
business being there had penetrated to the loading
platform and bludgeoned Tony to death with a

weapon he must have known was waiting there to be used. What had Tony missed? Who knew that he would eventually go to the loading platform on the way to picking up his car, a daily routine for him for a good ten years?

Chambrun and Jerry Dodd and I left the gruesome business of dealing with Tony Camargo's remains to Homicide and went back up to the Man's plush office on the second floor. We took Jimmy Heath, Tony's teary-eyed assistant, along with us.

Chambrun's face was carved out of stone as he sat at his desk, sipping some of his ghastly Turkish coffee. Miss Ruysdale stood behind his chair, waiting for orders. Nobody spoke. It was Chambrun's ball game.

"I don't want to scare you to death, Jimmy," he said after a moment, his bright black eyes narrowed against the smoke from his cigarette. "We have a story from Tony about the closing up of the Health Club last night. I'm convinced he missed something in telling us about it. I'm convinced he was killed to keep him from remembering what he missed and telling us about it."

"Oh, Jesus!" Jimmy Heath whispered.

"Tony told us you were with him during that final checkout."

"We always check out together," Jimmy said. "It saves time."

"You see why you should be afraid?"

"No, sir. Afraid of what?"

"You may remember what you missed, and before you can tell us you may be the next one on the murderer's list."

Jimmy stared at Chambrun, two great tears running down his cheeks. "There—there's nothing to remember," he stammered. "It—it was a routine checkout."

"The body was there this morning. How did it get there?"

"God only knows!" Jimmy said.

"There are only two avenues to explore," Chambrun said. "The body was either hidden in the club before you closed up and you overlooked it, or—"

"That just couldn't have happened, Mr. Chambrun," Jimmy cut in. "No way! We covered every square inch of the place—the pool, the rest rooms, the massage rooms, the steam room, the showers, the gym, the dressing cubicles, the johns, the office. No way that kid's body could have been there."

"Then we have to assume it was brought in after you and Tony had closed up and gone home," Chambrun said.

"It must be that way," Jimmy said.

"Which means you didn't lock up properly," Chambrun said.

"No sir!"

"Go over the routine for me."

"It's my job early on to bolt the fire doors," Jimmy said. "Then at the end, after the place has been cleaned up, the pool drained and refilled, the soiled linen carted out, the fresh linens put on the shelves, the dressing cubicles checked to make sure no customer has left anything behind in them or the johns, Tony and I walk through the joint and he double-checks the fire doors to make sure I haven't missed one. They were all bolted last night.''

"And then?''

"We check out the kitchen, go to the office, file away the clipboard sheet for the night in the cabinet there, take the front door keys from their hook on the wall—they're on the big ring with a plastic label—go to the front doors, set the two Yale-type locks on those doors so they'll lock when they close, go out in the hall and close them. They're locked. Then we try the doors to make sure the locks have caught.''

"And last night?''

"They were locked, Mr. Chambrun.

"We go down to the lobby with the keys and turn them over to the desk clerk on duty. Last night it was Chuck Dineen.''

"And then?''

"We're through,'' Jimmy said. "Sometimes Tony gives me a ride up to my apartment on the West Side in his Toyota. Sometimes we go our separate ways. Last night we split up. Tony had a date with some chick. I took a bus uptown and across town on 110th Street. I get off at Broadway which is only a block from where I have a room.''

"You know who the chick was Tony was dating?'' Chambrun asked.

"I don't know her last name,'' Jimmy said. "Mar-gradel something. She works in a bar down on Madison Avenue. He had real hot pants for her, but she was playing it cool. He had hopes last night was going to be it. That's why he was in a hurry to get going.''

''Being in a hurry he could have slipped up on something.''

''Not the fire doors, not the main doors,'' Jimmy insisted.

Chambrun looked around at the rest of us, as if to invite some kind of a question from one of us.

''Let's get realistic about this,'' Jerry Dodd said. ''Hardy hasn't been able to determine yet where the Sands boy was killed. You'd have to guess it was up in the club. You can't lug a dead body around this hotel any time of day or night. Customers and guests coming and going from the various bars and the Blue Lagoon until after three in the morning. Then cleaning and maintenance people everywhere. You don't carry a dead boy in your hip pocket. So let's say the killer persuaded the boy, somehow, to go up to the fourteenth floor with him. He must have known where he was going to take the boy. He didn't just find a door that was unlocked—if Jimmy's right about the close up.''

''Then he had to have keys to the main doors,'' Chambrun said. ''And if the Sands boy was taken up to the club alive, shot when they were inside, why hasn't Hardy found any trace of it? The kid must have bled like a stuck pig.''

Jerry's eyes were narrow slits. He had a theory that made sense. ''So the killer gets the boy into the club, takes him to the shower room, and shoots him in one of the shower stalls. He leaves him there to bleed. After a while he carries the body into the pool and dumps it. Then he goes back to the shower stall and washes all the evidence down the drain.''

''The bullet that went through that kid's head and came out the other side would have left a scar on the shower tiles,'' Chambrun said.

''I know,'' Jerry said. ''I'm going back up there right now to have a look. Hardy's people could have overlooked a mark on the tiles. The blood was washed away and the killer picked up the slug, but the scar will still be there.''

''If that's the way it happened,'' Chambrun said. ''Interesting theory, Jerry. Check it out.''

Jerry took off on a run. Something was itching at me, and I told Chambrun what it was.

''The killer had to have keys if Jimmy's right about the locking up last night,'' I said.

''I tell you it was locked tight,'' Jimmy said.

''So, as Jerry suggested, the killer had to know where he was taking the boy and how to get in.''

''There are duplicate keys, aren't there?'' Betsy Ruysdale asked.

''There are duplicate keys to every door in this hotel that has a lock on it,'' Chambrun said. ''Those duplicates, as you know, thousands of them, are kept in a walk-in safe in the front office. You don't just ask for them and get them. They're vital to our security.'' Chambrun crushed out his cigarette. ''But they exist,'' he said.

I knew that key safe. It was a large armor-plated room back of the front desk with a bank-vault door on it which could only be opened if you had the combination.

"Do you remember turning in the keys to Mr. Dineen last night, Jimmy?" Chambrun asked.

"Sure. Tony and I went to the desk, handed the key ring with the two keys on it to Chuck Dineen," Jimmy said.

"Was he busy at the time? I mean with customers, guests?"

"I don't remember that he was," Jimmy said. "No, he wasn't. Because he made some crack to Tony about how he looked 'pretty bushy-tailed' tonight. Tony said he hoped a certain young lady would find him irresistible. Mr. Dineen took the keys and went back inside with them. No, he wasn't busy with people."

"It's an unpleasant thought," I said, "but if the killer had keys to the Health Club someone on the inside must have sold us out, boss."

Chambrun looked at me as if I'd told him a tasteless dirty joke. "I don't buy that," he said, anger in his tone. "Not now, I hope not ever."

He trusted *his* people.

In the next hour I remember thinking that the early stages of a murder investigation—and I'd been in on several of them in my time at the Beaumont—are a little like bowling in some crazy alley where you knock down the pins and they pop right back up into place. Jerry Dodd's theory that the Sands boy might have been shot in a shower stall in the Health Club and the bloody evidence washed down the drain didn't prove out, at least not the way he'd hoped it would. He couldn't find a scar in any of the shower stalls that might have been made by the expanding bullet that had gone through the boy's skull.

Jerry, obviously disappointed, reported to Chambrun that there wasn't a scar, a chipped tile, anything that would support his theory.

"I know that kind of weaponry, boss," Jerry said. "That bullet would have gone through the boy's head with such force it would *have* to leave a mark. Hell, it could have ricocheted clean across the room. No way it wouldn't leave a mark on the tiles a couple of feet back of where it exited from the boy's skull."

"So, it was an interesting idea," Chambrun said.

The idea didn't entirely die there, however, because of evidence Hardy brought to the office about five that afternoon, while we were still knocking down pins that kept popping back into place. Hardy had discovered how the killer had gotten into the Health Club, either to murder Eddie Sands or to dispose of his body.

"Duplicate keys," the lieutenant told us.

"Not possible," Chambrun said stubbornly. No one could have gotten keys without some kind of betrayal in the front office. Chambrun was prepared to trust his three clerks, each of whom worked an eight-hour shift, right down to the end of the line. Andy Atwater, Chuck Dineen, and Karl Nevers had been trusted people for most of two decades.

"Not your duplicate keys," Hardy said, aware of the stubborn set to Chambrun's jaw. "I've got a lab report here, Pierre." He reached down and put a sheet of typed paper down on Chambrun's desk. "We examined the keys that are used every day, the ones on the large ring with the plastic label." He glanced at Jimmy Heath. "The keys Camargo and Heath turned into the front office at the end of their shift last night. There are traces of some kind of moulding wax on the key that fits the upper lock. They checked the lock itself and found a speck or two of the same wax in the lock."

"Someone made an impression of the keys on that ring and made his own duplicates?" Jerry Dodd asked.

Hardy nodded. "So it seems. It is possible the impression was taken sometime during the day, yesterday—on Carl Hulman's nine-to-five shift, or Camargo's five-to-ten shift. When Hulman got the keys back from the front desk this morning and opened up, that's when the specks of wax got in the lock. Unless you and Camargo used the keys when you locked up last night, Heath."

Jimmy shook his head. "We don't use the keys to lock up," he said. "We just set the locks, close the doors, test them from the outside. They lock themselves!"

"Where are the keys kept during the day?" Hardy asked.

"They hang on a hook in the office," Jimmy said. "Hulman gets them from the front desk when he gets here in the morning. He unlocks those front doors with them, hangs them up in the office, there's no reason for anyone to use them again until Tony and I take them back down to the front desk at night."

"They just hang there?"

"Yes, sir."

"Then any number of people in the course of a day could have access to them," Hardy said. "Can you make a guess as to how many people may have used the Health Club from the time it opened on Friday morning until the time Camargo and Heath closed it up on Friday night?"

"He doesn't have to guess," Chambrun said. He knew every detail of every routine in the Beaumont.

"Mr. Chambrun's right," Jimmy said. "Every guest or member who uses the club signs in on that clipboard sheet. Or is signed in, I should say. The clipboard sheets for Hulman's shift on Friday and Tony's and mine for the late afternoon and evening will tell you exactly how many and who they were. Friday isn't the busiest day on our shift—people leaving town for the weekend."

"Your staff signs in, too—the masseurs, the gym men, the squash pro?"

"And the lifeguard for the pool," Jimmy said. "We all sign in on a separate sheet in the office. That's filed away, too, and passed on to the business office on Mondays when the paychecks are made out."

"I want both those sets of records," Hardy said.

"I can get them for you if you like," Jimmy said.

It turned out Hulman had sixty-two users of the club on his Friday daytime shift. Camargo had only twenty-six, less than half his usual number on other nights.

"Any one of these people, plus the staff for both shifts, could have gotten to the keys," Hardy said, glancing down the list of names that could have been a sort of aristocracy of midtown business, plus some pretty fancy out-of-town guests, plus two work shifts of regular employees.

Jimmy Heath, who had brought the list down from the club, shook his head. "There's always someone in that little office, to check in the members and guests, to man the telephone. Theoretically it's Hulman during the day shift and Tony in the evening. If Hulman needs to leave the office to solve some kind of problem, or just to go to the john, Babe Triandos, his assistant, sits in for him. If Tony has to leave the office I sit in for him. If anyone was going to fool with those keys, there is no way it could be done without Hulman or Babe or Tony or me knowing it."

"Did you sit in for Tony at all on Friday night?" Hardy asked.

"No, sir. Friday night, about eight-thirty, Mr. Shuttleworth came in. He's a regular member and he wanted to play squash. You'll see his name on the list. The squash pro was already in one of the courts playing with Mr. Fessler, another member," Jimmy pointed to the list of names. "I can play well enough to give Mr. Shuttleworth a game so I went into the other court with him. We were still playing when the warning bell sounded. I suppose we'd been in the court for forty-five minutes."

"So you don't know whether Tony left the office or not?"

Jimmy looked uncomfortable. "No, sir. But now that you bring it up, I guess I should tell you that toward the end of our shift—after a quarter to nine, say—no one ever comes in to go through the routine. It takes about an hour to undress, exercise, shower and get a rubdown, and dress again—even without a rest period or time under the sun lamps. In that last forty-five minutes it wouldn't be too unusual for the office not to be covered. Tony might be starting to check out some of the closing details."

"And last night you were in the squash court so you wouldn't know for sure?"

"I suppose not," Jimmy said.

"And we can't ask Camargo," Hardy said, scowling.

"He had a date," Chambrun said. "He told us that, you told us that. He could have been in a hurry to get started with the close up."

"I suppose so," Jimmy said. "But in a way that was true at the end of our shift any night."

"So we have a time when someone could have gotten at the keys," Hardy said. "Can you tell us what members or guests were still in the club when you went into the squash court?"

"There could only have been about six or seven," Jimmy said. He glanced down the clipboard list. The names, of course, were in the chronological order of arrivals. The last six or seven names were probably the last six or seven users in that last forty-five minutes. The list ended with Tony Camargo's initials at the bottom—T.C.—indicating that that was that.

"Obviously there are addresses and phone numbers for these last users of the club last night," Hardy said.

"In a card file in the office," Jimmy said. "But you don't think any one of the members could have been at the keys?"

"The members have to go past the office when they're leaving?" Hardy asked.

"Only way out," Jimmy said.

"Then any one of the last eight or ten names who left the club may have seen someone in the office. It's wide open, just a counter on the entrance area."

"Yes, sir. If you walked by the office you could see anyone who might be in the office."

"It's a tedious business, but we're going to have to check with all the last people to leave the club, plus the staff who might have noticed someone."

"Tedious and lengthy," Chambrun said. He moved restlessly in his chair. "Saturday afternoon, half these people or more will have left town for the weekend."

"But you keep the club open on Saturday," Hardy said. "Hulman came in this morning when he found Sands' body."

"But we close up at the end of the day shift on Saturday," Chambrun said. "Camargo and Jimmy and their crew don't work on Saturdays. You'll be lucky,

Walter, if you can contact all these people before Monday or even Tuesday.''

"Well, it's got to be done," Hardy said. "Can you take me up and get those address cards for me, Heath?"

"Yes, sir."

"As for myself, I don't choose to sit here and twiddle my thumbs," Chambrun said.

Hardy, who had started for the door, turned back. He knew Chambrun from the past. "You hatching an egg, Pierre?" he asked.

"I'm unhappily back at square one," Chambrun said. "What brought Eddie Sands to the Beaumont? Did he arrive here alive or was he brought here dead? This wasn't just a mugging, Walter, it was planned, planned, planned! Nor do I intend to wait for Mr. Anonymous to throw us another red herring!"

"That sonofabitch calls us again we'll nail him to the wall," Hardy said. "If you have a vision, Pierre, let me in on it."

TWO

CHAMBRUN HADN'T HAD a vision, but he had a plan of action and it involved me. Betsy Ruysdale, Jerry Dodd, and I were left alone with him after Hardy went off with Jimmy to check his list.

"Somewhere down in Greenwich Village, not far from Jane Street, there's a stickball game going on," Chambrun said. He glanced at his wrist watch. "Five-thirty. There'll be three more hours of daylight. If I know kids they'll be playing as long as it's light. They are Eddie Sands' friends. He probably played with them yesterday afternoon. Did he play the usual time? When did he leave? Did he say anything about going to watch Stan Nelson's telethon? Somewhere there's a takeoff point."

"Got you," Jerry said. "I'm on my way."

"Not you, Jerry," Chambrun said. "Send a cop down there and these kids will clam up. Cops are the enemy these days. Send someone who looks like a cop—and that's you, Jerry—and they'll still clam up. It has to be Ruysdale or Mark." He gave the handsome Miss Ruysdale a thin smile. "They might be embarrassed to talk to a chick. So you're elected, Mark. I think you could pass as an amiable family friend."

"That's my profession, looking friendly. I'm not fond of kids," I said.

"Pretend," Chambrun said. "And after you've got whatever there is to get you won't be far from Forty-four Jane Street. Nora Sands asked you for help, maybe she'd be willing to give you some in exchange. I take it you wouldn't find that unpleasant."

Betsy Ruysdale laughed. "But hellishly dangerous from what I heard on the intercom," she said.

"Seriously," Chambrun said. "I think she wants what we do—a killer."

The curious thing about the Sands situation was that Nora Sands had not actually seen her son, who lived with her, since Thursday night. He had come home Thursday night after his stickball game and before she went to work at the Private Lives Club. He had made his own breakfast on Friday morning while she was still "at work." He had, Nora supposed, gone to school. He hadn't come home before she went to work on Friday night. That, Nora had told us, was not unusual. He played stickball late on Fridays because there was no school on Saturday and he had no homework to do. So Nora never saw her son from Thursday night until Saturday morning when Hardy pulled back the tarpaulin from his mangled face at the poolside in the Health Club. My job, in effect, was to find out how Eddie Sands had spent that Friday, what his pattern had been, what had eventually brought him to the Beaumont, which was way off his normal beat.

At today's prices you don't cruise around the city in a taxi cab. I took one of the Beaumont's private cars and headed downtown to the Village. A friendly cop, somewhere in the neighborhood of Sheridan Square, told me where I could find the nightly stickball game— on Thirteenth Street over near Ninth Avenue. The kids were at it under a full head of steam when I parked my car down the block and sauntered toward the game. The people in the neighborhood seemed to have given up any effort to avoid the shouts and screams of excitement, and most of the front steps of the old houses had become a kind of bleachers for those people too old to play.

Stickball is played with a rubber ball, and the bats appear to be made from old broom handles. A fire hydrant was first base; the top off a wooden crate was second base; an overturned garbage can was third. The pitcher throws the ball up to the hitter on one bounce, and I guess, if you're good at it, you can make the ball take some crazy bounces. They obviously had their own special ground rules. A ball hit fair above the second-floor level of one of the buildings was a home run. A ball hit off a building below that was in play, no matter where it careened to. The kids were playing with such enthusiasm and intensity, punctuated by violent arguments, that I couldn't see just how I was going to get to talk to any of them, at least while they were still at it.

Then I spotted a young black boy, probably about Eddie Sands' age, sitting on one of the front steps. He was an enthusiastic rooter, probably a player who was for the moment a wounded warrior. His right ankle was in a cast and a pair of crutches rested on the brownstone steps beside him. I sat down on the step just below him.

"Who's who?" I asked him.

He gave me a quick look out of bright brown eyes and decided I was safe. "East of Eighth Avenue and west of Eighth Avenue," he said.

"How did you hurt your ankle?"

"Broke it sliding into the pushcart," he said.

"The pushcart?"

"Old man Weimer's pushcart is third base on Tuesday night," the boy said.

Someone hit a screaming liner down the middle of Thirteenth Street, and the center fielder let it get past him. It was going to be an inside-the-park homer. There were shouts of delight but my young friend pounded the knee on his good leg with both fists.

"Playin' too far in," he said. "I told him." He glanced at me. "I'm the regular center fielder for the west side. That jerk never played there before."

We watched the next hitter being thrown out in a close play to the fire hydrant.

"Jane Street is east of here," I said casually. "Eddie Sands must have played for the east team." He swiveled around to look at me. "Was he any good?"

The brown eyes narrowed. "You some kind of a cop?" he asked.

I grinned at him. "Do I look like one?"

After a moment he shook his head. Score one for Chambrun.

"I'm a friend of Eddie's mother," I said. Well, she had asked me for help! "You got a name?"

"Norman," he said.

"First or last?"

"First—what else?"

"Were you here last Friday, Norman?"

"Every night they play."

"Eddie played?"

"Sure. I didn't, because of my ankle. Eddie was the best hitter the east had."

"You know what's happened to him?"

"You'd have to be deaf not to hear it on the radio all day," Norman said. "Do they know who yet?"

"No. Nor why, Norman. That's why I'm nosing around. He didn't go home in time for his mother to see him before she went to work on Friday night."

"We had a hamburger roast after the game last night," Norman said. "Eddie stuck around."

"That would have been after dark."

"We play till we can't see anymore," Norman said. "When the street lights come on we quit."

"You talk to Eddie at all?"

"After the game," Norman said. "He was a nice guy. He brought me a burger, because I couldn't move around easy, and a Pepsi."

"Talk about anything special—like going to watch Stan Nelson's telethon at the Beaumont?"

"I guess you didn't know Eddie too well," Norman said.

"Meaning?"

"If you did you'd know he wouldn't go to hear Stan Nelson sing if they paid him for it. Eddie didn't like that kind of music. He was a rock fan. Collected rock records. Never listened to anything else but.''

"Did he tell you how he was going to spend the evening?''

"He didn't say. I've been trying to remember, ever since the news came on the radio. He didn't say. He was mostly worried about his key.''

"Key?''

"He lost the key to his apartment. He looked all over the street for it after the game. It must have come out of his pocket when he slid into a base or something. Anyhow, he'd lost it and he couldn't find it.''

"He was worried because he couldn't get into his apartment?''

"Naw,'' Norman said. "He could always go up the fire escape and get into his place. But he was afraid his old lady would be sore at him for losing his key.''

"And he didn't tell you what he planned to do with the rest of his evening?''

"No reason he should,'' Norman said. "He didn't cowboy around like some of us on Friday nights. He'd usually go home, listen to records, read. He was a great reader.''

"Girls?''

Norman shook his head. "Eddie wasn't much for girls. Don't get me wrong, I'm not saying he was gay. I guess you could say the fire hadn't got lit under him yet.''

I smiled at the boy. "Not like you,'' I suggested.

He rolled his eyes up. "Oh, man!'' he said.

"So the last you saw of Eddie last night he was headed home—to climb up his fire escape and spend the evening listening to records and reading?"

"Look, mister, he didn't say that's what he was going to do. He didn't say what he was going to do, except that when he *did* go home he'd have to go up the fire escape."

"So you don't think he had a date?"

"With a chick? Not Eddie."

"Do any of the kids play cards, or other games, after it's too dark to play stickball?"

"Not Eddie. He was a kind of loner, except for these east-west games. Sometimes in summer his old lady would give him a few extra bucks and he'd go to Shea Stadium or Yankee Stadium to see a real ball game. He was a real freak for baseball. But not last night. Last night he was just worrying about his lost key."

We were, I thought, suddenly living in a world of keys.

NORMAN HAD BEEN FRIENDLY enough but he hadn't advanced me very far. Up till dark on Friday night Eddie Sands had followed a usual routine. If he'd had any special plans for after the stickball game he hadn't confided them to Norman.

I left the stickball game, still going strong, and went back to my car. The second part of my job was to talk to Nora Sands in the hope that she might have come up with something useful now that the shock of Eddie's death was a few hours old.

I drove east to Jane Street and found myself in the middle of some kind of excitement there. Three police cars and an ambulance were parked on the north side of the street, and a small crowd of people were milling around. I parked and walked along the street to where number 44 should be. When I got there I found that number 44 was the center of whatever was going on. A cop was standing in the doorway, and the people outside were looking up at the upper windows.

The cop stopped me as I started to go into the building.

"You live here?" he asked me.

"No. Just calling on a friend," I told him.

"What friend?" He was a tough-looking cookie.

"Miss Sands—if it's any of your business," I said.

"It's my business," the cop said. "Just stand aside a minute."

From inside the building came the ambulance crew, carrying someone on a stretcher. I couldn't get a glimpse of the sick or injured person. The stretcher was rolled into the ambulance and it took off, siren wailing.

Two other men had followed the stretcher from the house. One of them was obviously a plainclothes cop, the other was a handsome guy, well over six feet, wearing a tan gabardine suit, white shirt and tie, nicely polished brown shoes.

"What I have here, Sergeant," the cop said, "is a gentleman caller." He suddenly had hold of my arm with fingers.

The plainclothes cop gave me an ice-blue stare. "I'm Sergeant Keller, Ninth Precinct," he said. "Your name, please."

"What the hell is this?" I said.

"Your name, Buster!" the uniformed cop said, and his fingers bit into my arm so hard my knees buckled.

"My name is Mark Haskell," I said.

"Address?"

"I'm the public relations director for the Beaumont Hotel, I live there."

Keller's ice-blue eyes narrowed. "You've had a couple of homicides up there today. You were calling on Miss Sands?"

"I *am* calling on Miss Sands," I said.

"You'll have to try St. Vincent's Hospital," Keller said. "That was Miss Sands they just took off in the ambulance. You got any I.D. on you, Mr. Haskell?"

"I have. And if you want a character reference you might try Lieutenant Hardy of Manhattan Homicide."

"I will," Keller said.

"What happened to her?" I asked, as I handed him my wallet, complete with driver's license, Social Security card, and three different credit cards.

"Somebody broke in, beat her up badly, probably robbed the joint. It's torn to pieces." Keller glanced at my credentials and handed back my wallet. "Just a social call?" he asked.

I didn't like him. The cop had loosened his grip on my arm and I shook it free. "Some law against it?" I asked.

"Maybe there ought to be," Keller said.

I liked him even less. He was suggesting that I might be the customer of a high-class prostitute.

"I came down to this part of town, with the full knowledge of Lieutenant Hardy," I said, "to try to find some of Eddie Sands' friends—the kids he played stickball with. We were trying to trace out his day yesterday. His mother hadn't seen him since the day before. I talked to one of his friends, and then I came around here, hoping Miss Sands might have recovered enough to remember something that bypassed her this morning. I just walked up the front steps when Knucklehead here stopped me."

The cop reached for my arm again but I took a quick step away from him.

"I guess you're clean, Mr. Haskell," Keller said. "I'll know where to reach you if I need you." He turned to the tall man in the gabardine suit. "The same goes for you, Reverend."

Keller beckoned to the cop and they took off for one of the police cars. The tall guy held out his hand to me.

"I'm Len Martin," he said. He could have been a movie star, Gary Cooper type. Nicely tanned, fortyish I guessed. The way he gave me his name was as if I was supposed to know who he was. I took his hand. The grip was firm.

He saw that I'd drawn a blank. "The Reverend Leonard Martin, leader of the New Morality," he said.

I realized now where I'd seen him—TV news, newspapers. He was handsome enough to interest the press photographers. There are suddenly hundreds of these "morality" groups around the country. The Reverend Leonard Martin is one of the chief crusaders against sex, violence, and raunchy language on television. He's also made quite a splurge trying to close up porno bookstores and so-called massage parlors in the Times Square area.

"You're a friend of Nora Sands?" he asked me. He had a deep, resonant voice like you can produce with a foot pedal on an organ.

"I met her for the first time this morning when she came to the Beaumont, where I work, to identify the body of her murdered son."

"What a ghastly business," he said. "We live in a time when violence multiplies like... like..."

"Rabbits," I suggested.

He gave me a thin frown. I realized I'd suggested sex! You have to watch your step with the Reverend Leonard Martins of this world.

"You know more of what happened here than the police sergeant told me?" I asked him.

"I was, unluckily, the person who found her," Martin said. "Unlucky for me, perhaps lucky for her. I called the police and they sent an ambulance. The ambulance doctor doesn't think her chances are too good, but if there'd been much more delay he thinks she'd have had no chance at all."

"Was she able to talk?" I asked.

Martin shook his head. "Beaten senseless," he said. "First thing I did was feel for a pulse. It was almost nonexistent."

"How did you happen to be the one to find her?"

He looked down at his hands. I saw that his finger-nails were well manicured. "I take it you know some-thing about the work I do," he said.

"You manage to get plenty of publicity, Mr. Mar-tin."

"Publicity is important in getting the general pub-lic, the people, lined up on our side," he said. "The police, the courts, the politicians aren't much help to us. We have to stir up public outrage to make any headway at all."

"What does that have to do with your finding Nora Sands?"

"I have been given a new assignment by the higher-ups in my organization," he said.

"I suppose you were the top man," I said.

"I am, I suppose you would say, the out-front man," he said. "I take my orders from a council of elders. My job at the moment is to focus on, close down if possible, the pornographic empire of a man named Zachary Thompson. You've heard of *Private Lives Magazine* and the Private Lives clubs scattered all over the country?"

"I know about them, of course. I had the dubious pleasure of meeting Zach Thompson only this morn-ing. He came to the hotel to help Nora Sands."

He nodded. "He makes a pretense of 'taking care' of his people. I have, in the past few weeks, been fo-cusing my attention on the Private Lives Club here in the Village."

"As a customer?" I have to admit I don't have a very high opinion of these professional moral crusaders. They go to all the raunchy movies, watch all the sex and violence on TV, read all the porno books, and then tell the rest of us we must lay off. I remember talking to Chambrun about it once and he said they appeared to be "on a Peeping Tom road to Heaven. What fun!" I have never cottoned to having someone tell me what I should read, or look at, or drink, or whether I should make love to a lady who attracts me, in or out of wedlock! It's my life and I don't want it dictated to by a Big Brother. The Reverend Leonard Martin, hanging around with Zach Thompson's Private Lives girls and then expressing his outrage, seemed somewhat grotesque to me. I could be wrong about him, I knew. He could be on the level, a genuine do-gooder, but I didn't want his code of morals imposed on me.

"The glamor of the Private Lives clubs is a cover for open prostitution," Martin said. "The authorities pay no attention to it. I meant to—I mean to—work up a legal case against them that they can't sidestep."

"Let's go back a few yards," I said. "You say you found Nora Sands upstairs here in her apartment, near death."

"Nora is called a 'hostess' at the Private Lives Club," he said. I had the feeling he was trying to justify some action of his. "In my father's day she would have been called 'the madam.' Thompson knows that I'm out to get him."

"And yet you're welcomed as a customer?"

"It's a public place," Martin said. "It's not like an old-fashioned speakeasy where you have to have a password to get in. The first time I went there Thompson spotted me. He knew why I was there and yet he rolled out a red carpet for me. I could see, or go anywhere in the club I wanted. Nora Sands was turned over to me as a guide and question-answerer. Drinks were on the house except that I don't drink. Coffee and sandwiches were courtesy of the management. Nora—Miss Sands—couldn't have been a more gracious hostess. It took me a while to realize that the regular goings-on had come to a dead stop while I was there. Nora wanted me to believe that it was just a place where lonely men could find pleasant company—a few drinks, a little food, a pretty girl to talk to, maybe to dance with. In the process of trying to sell me on a lie I came to realize that Nora was an extraordinary woman, warm, with wit and humour, concerned with raising a son she admitted was illegitimate. I knew what she had been and what she was, but I couldn't help liking her, wishing I could—could turn her life around, set her on the road to salvation." He hesitated a moment. "I'm afraid I lost sight of my main objective for a while. Nora became my cause, almost without my realizing it I wanted to get her away from there, to set her on a new road, to supply her with new values."

"And you wound up in the hay with her?"

"No!" he almost shouted. "But—but I have to admit to you, Haskell, the temptation was there. I had to stop going to the club, stop seeing her. I came as close as I will ever come to breaking my vows, to abandoning my principles.''

I could imagine Nora had made it rough for him. She needed sex ''like air,'' she'd told me. A man would have to be a saint to turn his back on her if she baited her hook for him.

''I was sitting in my study this afternoon, trying to make plans to attack Thompson somewhere else, in some other city, some other area, when I turned on my radio and heard the news that Nora's son had been found murdered in your hotel. I knew that this must be a total devastation for her. I had the feeling there were no real friends she could turn to. Thompson and the people in the club couldn't offer her any real comfort, help to bolster her courage, turn her in God's direction in a time of terrible need. I—I tried to call her on the phone but it was perpetually busy. I finally persuaded an operator to help me and got the word that her phone was out of service, probably the receiver had been left off the hook. And so—so I came over here.'' Martin took a deep breath. ''She didn't answer the doorbell but the main door was open, so I walked up the two flights to her apartment.''

''You knew where it was?''

He gave me a steady look. ''Yes, I knew where it was. Nora had invited me here for supper one Sunday—her day off.''

''A good chance to put her on the road to salvation,'' I said.

The Reverend Leonard Martin wasn't a dummy. He sensed my antagonism to him and his ''message.'' ''I guess we live in different worlds, Mr. Haskell," he said.

"I'm just interested in knowing how you came to find Nora Sands," I said.

He nodded. "As I said, she didn't answer her doorbell, but this street-level front door was open. I could see the building superintendent mopping the floor at the rear of the front hall. I asked him if he knew if Nora was in. He just shrugged and said he had no idea. I—I went up to the third floor where her apartment is. I was about to knock when I saw the door was standing open an inch or two." He took a deep breath. "I pushed the door open a little wider and called out to her. No answer, but I got a glimpse of her living room. It was a shambles, Mr. Haskell. Furniture tipped over, couch cushions ripped apart by a knife or something, books thrown out of the cases onto the floor, drawers pulled out of her desk and dumped on the floor. I—I called out to her again. No answer. And so I—I walked through the mess to the little hall that leads to her bedroom and bath." His breathing came harder. "There was the same crazy destruction in the bedroom, plus—plus Nora, lying half on and half off the bed, covered with blood, her face terribly bruised and bleeding. I went to her. Unconscious. I—I felt for a pulse and it was almost not there. The phone was lying on the floor, receiver off the hook. I could hear the steady dial tone. I dialed 911, the police emergency number, reported what I'd found, and waited for help to come." He took a white handkerchief out of his breast pocket and blotted at the little beads of sweat that had appeared on his forehead.

"You didn't try to get help from anyone in the building—the super or other tenants?" I asked him.

"I—I have been trained in first aid," Martin told me. "I was afraid she was going. I—I tried mouth-to-mouth to get her breathing a little better. I got a wet cloth from the bathroom to try to clean up her face. Her eyelids fluttered a little. She was still trying to make it. The police and the ambulance responded very quickly—eight or nine minutes, I would guess. Cops are up there now, trying to find something that will give them a clue to the attacker. He must have handled nearly everything in the apartment. There must be fingerprints—something."

"When she comes to—" I said.

"I don't think they think she will come to," Martin said. "I think I'll go to St. Vincent's and see if there's any news."

"I'll drive you there," I said. "I have a car parked down the block."

It took about ten minutes to get to the hospital and find a parking place. The waiting room outside the emergency room was crowded with a strange assortment of people; a wailing Hispanic woman whose son was behind the closed doors suffering from a knife wound received in a street brawl, a young woman whose child was a hit-and-run victim, an old man whose wife had suffered a heart attack—and on and on. The desk informed us that Nora Sands was still in the emergency surgery, in the care of one Dr. Morgan.

"You'll have to wait for Dr. Morgan to come out to get any report," the girl at the desk told us.

"Long?" Martin asked her.

"Depends on the patient. Could be minutes, could be hours."

"I'll wait," Martin said.

He may have been a phony, but he was also a friend, I told myself. I had to find a phone to get back to Chambrun. He may already have heard about Nora, but I had to be sure.

The pay phone was in an outer hall. I started for it when my attention was called to a man sitting on one of the waiting benches. He was looking directly at me, giving me a bright, white-toothed smile. He was, I thought, probably about thirty. He was dark-skinned, possibly Hispanic, or a black Irishman, or an Italian. He was wearing a baseball cap with a Yankee insignia on it, the kind they give away free at certain ball games, jeans, an orange sport shirt, blue sneakers. The smile suggested that he knew me, but I drew a partial blank. It was partial because there was something vaguely familiar about him. If I hadn't felt it was so urgent to get to Chambrun I might have stopped to speak to him, to place him; I didn't, and I was to regret it.

You have to understand that the nature of my job at the Beaumont brought me into contact with hundreds of different people every day of my life. They come and go to register as guests, to eat in the restaurants, to drink in the bars, to patronize the Blue Lagoon, our night club. Hundreds of faces become familiar without my knowing who they are or anything about them. The man in the baseball cap didn't look like a patron of the hotel. I decided he'd made some kind of mistake in thinking that he knew me.

Chambrun had heard about Nora. Sergeant Keller had been in touch with Hardy. There was more. There'd been another phone call from Mr. Anonymous. *"Stan Nelson is rich enough to hire an army of hit-men. He sits calmly in your hotel while he arranges to exterminate the Sands family."*

"Were you able to trace the call?" I asked Chambrun.

"A pay phone on the corner of Greenwich Avenue and Jane Street," Chambrun told me. "Right there in the neighborhood where you are. The cops were too late."

"Damn!" I said. "What next, boss?"

I'd told him about Norman, my stickball friend, and the Reverend Leonard Martin. "Stay where you are for a while," Chambrun said. "See who comes inquiring for Miss Sands. I think you can expect Zachary Thompson. Who else?"

"If she dies without talking?"

"Then we're back at square one," Chambrun said. "Get your reverend friend to start praying."

I went back to rejoin my reverend friend in the waiting room. The man in the baseball cap was gone.

STAYING ANCHORED in the waiting room outside that emergency ward with the wails of that Hispanic mother reaching ear-piercing crescendos from time to time is not a way I recommend for passing time. There wasn't any way to carry on a conversation without making it so loud it would become everyone's business. Leonard Martin sat erect on the bench next to me, staring straight ahead at the opposite wall. There was nothing to look at there except a poster asking you to support your local blood bank. Maybe he *was* praying.

We'd been there about forty-five minutes when Chambrun's forecast came true. Zachary Thompson made a flamboyant entrance accompanied by a sexy-looking dark-haired girl who couldn't have been more than twenty. I was reminded of the girls who advertise jeans on television. She was wearing jeans, tight around the hips and a curvaceous behind, and a blue man's shirt unbuttoned down to there in front. They barged up to the desk where Thompson poked his bearded face almost into the receptionist's and demanded to know where Nora Sands was and how he could get to her. He was told she was in Emergency, not seeable. He drowned out the wailing lady with his demands. He must talk to someone in authority. He had a right to be with Nora, whatever she was going through. The receptionist, apparently used to loud voices and hysteria, promised she would find someone he could talk to. He'd have to wait. He spun away and spotted the Reverend Martin staring at the blood donor poster. He was almost on top of us before he appeared to recognize me. I guess I didn't matter to him.

"You found her, Martin!" Thompson shouted.

Martin seemed to come out of a kind of trance. I thought for a moment he actually didn't recognize Thompson, but then his thin mouth tightened.

"Yes, I found her," he said. "I heard on the radio about her son. I went to see if I could be of any help. I found her."

"How bad is it, Mr. Martin?" the dark-haired girl asked.

He looked at her. "You are—?"

"Linda," she said.

"Ah, yes," Martin said. He had obviously met her in his "work" at the Private Lives Club. "It is not good, I'm afraid," he said. "Not good at all. The ambulance doctor wasn't sure he could get her here alive, but he did. We're waiting. They say it could be hours before they know."

"What doctor has she got?" Thompson demanded.

"Someone on the staff, I suppose. A Dr. Morgan."

"I know him!" Thompson said. He turned and headed back for the receptionist.

The girl watched him go, and then turned to Martin. "Dr. Morgan has helped us out at the club now and then—a customer had a heart attack once, one of the girls will turn up sick now and then. He has a private office just around the corner from the club."

"I'm Mark Haskell," I told her. "I'm waiting to hear about Nora, too. You're Linda what?"

"Just Linda," the girl said.

"The girls at the club don't have last names," Martin said. "The customers might try to see them without Thompson sharing in the profits."

"It's for our own protection," Linda said. She seemed unperturbed by Martin's suggestion that she was a prostitute. Maybe she just saw it as a fact of life. She looked at me. "You know Nora?"

"For a very short time," I said.

"She's the nicest person I ever met," Linda said. "She'll help you out of any kind of trouble. She's kind and generous. She's even loaned me money a couple of times when I was broke. And poor little Eddie! My God, Mr. Haskell, what kind of a world is this?"

"We make the world we live in," Martin said.

Linda looked at him and for a moment I saw anger. "She was even nice to you, Mr. Martin, though she knew you were trying to do her harm."

"I was trying to save her from a terrible judgment," Martin said.

"You know something, Mr. Martin?"

"What?"

"You're some kind of creep!" Linda said.

"My values are different from yours, child," he said. "Perhaps, someday, you and I can—"

She laughed at him. "You have to be kidding!" she said.

I found I rather liked Linda.

Zach Thompson came back from the receptionist's desk. "That stupid broad has finally got me to someone who has some authority. Wait here, Linda."

Linda watched him disappear into the bowels of the hospital. "You'd be surprised how many doors he can get to open up for him," she said. She didn't, of course, have any idea how close to home that comment hit. Someone with a gift for opening doors had got into the Health Club at the Beaumont, into Nora Sands' apartment on Jane Street, into a restricted area in the basement of the hotel. Of course Linda hadn't meant opening doors in that literal sense.

At that moment a man in a green doctor's suit and surgical cap came out of the emergency room. He went to the desk and the receptionist pointed to Martin. The doctor came over to us.

"Reverend Martin?"

Martin stood up and held out his hand. The doctor ignored it, flexing his hand as though it hurt in advance. "I'm Dr. Morgan," he said. Then he noticed Linda. "You're from the Private Lives Club, aren't you?"

"Yes, Dr. Morgan. Zach's here, looking for you. I guess he went to see the boss, the king, whoever runs this place."

"He would!" Morgan said. He turned back to Martin. "I understand from the police that you found Miss Sands, Mr. Martin."

"Yes. How is she, Doctor?"

"Not good," Morgan said. "She didn't tell you anything when you found her?"

"She was unconscious."

"We'll be lucky if she ever tells anybody anything," Morgan said.

"That bad?" Linda asked, her voice unsteady.

"That bad," Morgan said. "I want to move her into a private room with special life-support systems. We are supposed to dispense mercy here, but unfortunately mercy costs money." He sounded bitter. "I have to assure the front office that someone will pay the freight."

"I'm sure Zach will take care of it," Linda said. "Nora's worked for him for a good many years. Zach never lets his people down."

"They have too much on him," the Reverend Martin said.

"You may have something there," Morgan said. "When he comes back ask him to go to the business office and tell them. I'm going to put him down as responsible for Miss Sands."

"Is there anything any of us can do?" Martin asked.

"If you've got a special pipeline to God, Mr. Martin, use it," the doctor said. He turned and walked away toward the emergency room.

Linda put a cold hand on top of mine. "Let's go have a drink somewhere," she said.

You DON'T HAVE TO GO very far in any direction in New York without finding a reasonably presentable bar. There was one directly across the street from the hospital, something a little better than a side-street dive. I suppose the families and friends of people who can afford to be sick want something better than sawdust on the floor.

I'm not quite sure why I decided to buy Linda a drink when I should have been on my way back to the Beaumont to give Chambrun a detailed report. Perhaps it was because she seemed to be genuinely fond of Nora Sands and badly shaken by what Dr. Morgan had told us about Nora's chances. I told myself it wasn't because she was a sexy-looking girl who just might be available. I guess I've mentioned that I'm not to be trusted about women who can be had. Some other time, perhaps. There was, I convinced myself, a legitimate reason for staying with her for a little. She knew Nora well, apparently knew Eddie Sands, knew Zach Thompson and his porno world. Perhaps, without realizing it, she could tell me why someone had set out to eliminate the Sands family and was trying to persuade the police that Stan Nelson, who just might have been Eddie Sands' father, was responsible.

We sat in a booth in the bar across from the hospital. A waitress came over and asked us if we wanted to eat or if we were just drinking. We weren't interested in food. Linda ordered a vodka and tonic, and I a Jack Daniels on the rocks with a splash of plain water.

Linda took a Kleenex from her handbag and dabbed at her eyes with it. I realized she'd been crying as we walked across the street.

"Is my mascara smeared?" she asked me.

"You look fine," I said.

She asked me about Eddie Sands, and I gave her a brief rundown. He'd been found in the pool in the Beaumont Health Club. Someone had made duplicates of the keys that opened the place and taken him there after everyone had left and the place was, theoretically, inaccessible.

"Both of them in one day!" she said.

"And that isn't all," I told her about Tony Camargo. "Beaten up much the same way Nora was beaten."

It obviously didn't make any more sense to her than it did to me.

"Do you know much about Nora's private life?" I asked her.

The waitress brought our drinks and Linda didn't say anything until we were alone again. "Nora wasn't like a lot of the girls who work at Private Lives. She was older, of course, and she'd been through it all long ago—I guess out on the coast where she worked in Zach's club out there. Sometimes she'd talk about one of the movie stars she'd known, some of the big-shot Hollywood executives. Now she's a sort of hostess-manager for Zach. He travels around a lot. There are seven other clubs, you know; Atlantic City, Miami Beach, Chicago, Houston, Tucson, New Orleans, Hollywood. The offices of *Private Lives Magazine* are in Hollywood, too. Zach has to keep an eye on all of them and he keeps moving around. We don't see him as often as some of the other places do. That's because he trusts Nora and she does such a good job of running the club here. If she can't work for a while I imagine he'll stay with us pretty steadily till she can. That we won't like too well."

"Why?"

She gave me a steady look, almost a defiant look. "I'm a prostitute, you know."

"I assume that's what working at a Private Lives club meant," I said.

"Working for Nora is different from working for Zach," she said. "You know how the club operates, Mark?"

"Tell me."

"A customer comes in. The girls are parading around in the lounge. There's music and drinks, of course. Customer picks out a girl he likes the looks of and that means, in the end, that you wind up in the hay with him."

"There in the club?"

"Oh, no. The cops would have nailed us long ago if that was the way it worked. Zach has eight or ten small apartments scattered around the Village. The same thing is true in the other cities, I guess. When the time for the payoff comes you take your customer to one of those apartments."

"At today's rental figures that sounds like an expensive operation," I said.

"We aren't two-dollar street hookers, Mark," she said. "The customer buys us for the night, pays at the club before we go anywhere with him."

"What makes working for Nora better than working for Thompson?" I asked her.

She looked away and I saw a little shudder move her shoulders. "You'd have to see them to believe some of the characters who come into the club to buy a woman," she said. "Some of them are just too much! If Zach's in charge you've got no choice. A customer picks you and you go with him, like it or not. You don't go and you're out on the street. Nora will give you a break. If you say you just can't take that one she'll tell the john you've been spoken for in advance. Sometimes he's a repeater. You've been out with him once and you wouldn't go again for all the tea in China. Nora will turn him on to someone else. There are a couple of girls who'll go with anyone if her cut is big enough. Nora is a woman who just likes sex, but as far as I know she picks her own people. She doesn't 'hire out' the way the rest of us do."

"Did she ever mention Stan Nelson to you?"

Linda's eyes widened. "It's funny you should ask that," she said. "Because it was only last night that she talked about him. We were in the dressing room before the night trade started to come in—about eight-thirty, I guess. I switched on the radio on my dressing table. Stan Nelson was singing a song—for that cancer telethon he does. 'Days of Wine and Roses,' it was. Nora gave me a funny smile. 'He's still the very best at what he does,' she said. It was as if she had some kind of personal feeling for it, not just a music lover. 'Would you believe that long ago, before Eddie was born, I lived with Stan for two whole years?' she told me. A big house, she told me, her own car, servants, trips to all the places he had singing dates if she wanted to go, access to movie lots when he was making a film. 'He was the nicest guy I've ever known,' she told me. I asked her why she let it break up. 'Because I couldn't stay out of bed with any other guy who came along when Stan was away working on a film. I have always been on sex the way other people are on hashish,' she told me. She gave me a funny look. 'It's just possible Stan could have been Eddie's father.' Well, that jolted me. 'Well was he or wasn't he?' I asked her. 'I don't honestly know,' she said. 'Zach helped me bring a suit against him for a property settlement. I lost the suit, but I could have won it if I'd been willing to say Stan was Eddie's father. He was too nice a guy for me to hang that kind of a rap on him.'" Linda looked at me. "Was Stan Nelson Eddie's father?"

"She told me just what she told you," I said.

"Did Eddie know Stan might be his father?"

"She said not."

"But he was up there at the telethon, with Stan's autograph in his pocket—according to the radio!"

"That we don't know for sure," I said. "Did Zach Thompson ever mention Stan to you?"

"Today, on the way to the hospital," Linda said. "The club isn't open to the public in the afternoons, but I was there because I had some clothes that needed ironing before tonight. I'd forgotten to leave them for our wardrobe woman and she leaves early on Saturdays. I had my radio on and the news came over about Nora being found by Leonard Martin beaten and unconscious." She gave me a bitter little smile. "Women in our business don't usually make the news when they get beat up. It goes with the territory.''

"Customers beat you up?" I asked, mildly shocked.

"Some of them get sexual kicks out of it," Linda said. "I guess the high mucky-mucks think we deserve whatever we get and it isn't news. But with Nora it was only hours after her son had been found murdered in the Beaumont, and Stan Nelson's name had been brought into that. Stan Nelson is news anytime, I guess. But you asked if Zach had mentioned him.''

"And you said 'just today.'''

"Well, when I heard the news about Nora I dropped everything and started to run out of the club to go to St. Vincent's. I thought there might be something I could do for Nora. Like I said, I really love that lady. She'd helped me often when I thought I'd come to the end of the line. I almost collided with Zach down in the lounge. He'd just heard the same broadcast I had and he was on his way. He took me with him in a taxi. I have to hand it to Zach. He stands by his people.''

I'd hear this before.

"He couldn't guess who had done this to Nora or why. But he said something like, 'Stan Nelson is probably sitting up there in the Beaumont, grinning from ear to ear. You can bet on it that sonofabitch doesn't wish Nora well.' I asked him why and he told me that Nora had once tried to sue Stan for half his property out in California. 'An elephant never forgets,' he said. 'Somebody knows and has been trying to put the police wise when Eddie was found, but the pigs won't lay a finger on Mr. Nice Guy.'''

"That was it?"

She nodded. "I remembered she'd told me Zach had helped her with her suit, and they'd lost it. Zach doesn't forgive anyone who beats him at anything. I figured if Nora had won her suit Zach would have shared in the proceeds. He wouldn't forgive that. He eats money for breakfast!"

"How big a cut does he take from you?" I asked her.

She gave me that steady, defiant look again, as if she was daring me to express disapproval. "I'm worth three hundred dollars a night," she said. "I get half of it and the club gets the other half. Unless it's a sting."

"What do you mean 'sting'?"

She hesitated. "A couple of these apartments I mentioned are equipped with video cameras."

I couldn't believe it. "They take pictures of you in the act?"

She nodded. "If the sucker is an important guy in politics, or socially, or some other kind of big wheel who can't afford scandal, I may be ordered to take him to one of those places—we call them 'picture palaces.' Afterwards the poor slob will pay off in big money to keep the wrong people from seeing what he's been up to."

"Organized blackmail!" I said.

"I get an extra piece of change if I'm used for one of those setups. I usually feel pretty lousy about it, but it's a living."

"Oh, brother!" I said.

"So you think I'm a bum, so say so!" she said.

"I think Thompson is a bum, a Grade A bastard!" I said.

She glanced down at her drink, which she hadn't touched after the first sip. "We don't have bear traps out in the street to catch the customers and drag them into the Private Lives Club," she said. "They come in of their own free will. They expect to buy something and it's there for them to buy. Believe me, most of them come because they like sex without having to make any commitments. They'd laugh at you if you threatened to tell someone. It's a sport they like, like golf, or tennis, or playing the horses. A small portion of them come, loaded with guilt, probably cheating on a rich wife. Would you believe a priest or a minister? Those are the suckers who will pay for silence, and Zach doesn't let them off the hook."

"I would have thought the amateur competition would take care of them. Where I work you can find a willing amateur in almost no time at all."

She gave me her hard little smile. "You a connoisseur, Haskell?"

"I've been around," I said.

"Maybe you don't know how much better we professionals are at what we do than all your amateur men chasers."

I think she saw from my face that I'd never paid for any lovemaking in my whole checkered career.

"You ought to try sometime," she said. "You might become a convert."

I wanted to get away from there. "You mentioned priests and ministers. What about the Reverend Leonard Martin?"

"A cop in lamb's clothing," she said. "He wanted so badly to trip up Zach Thompson's world you could almost see him tasting it. Zach let Nora handle him. She was far too smart for the reverend boob. I sometimes wondered if she hadn't hooked him and put him right over a barrel."

"The picture palace game?"

"She'd never set anyone up that way. That's Zach's game."

"Not Nora but the reverend obviously got so sweet on her he lost sight of what he was there to do. He got to be so intent on saving her from damnation that he forgot about wrecking Zach Thompson's business."

I had to get back to the Beaumont or Chambrun would have my head on the block. I could imagine Eliot Stevens and the rest of the media people yammering at him for news. My job was to protect him from that. I explained to Linda.

"There are going to be cops circulating around your club," I told her, "asking questions about Nora and Eddie. You haven't mentioned Eddie but you sounded as if you knew and liked him."

"He was a sweet kid," Linda said. "I never saw him much because Nora wouldn't let him come to the club. It's no place for a teenage boy or a younger kid. But some Sundays Nora would invite me to her place for a late afternoon brunch. That's breakfast time for us after a Saturday night. Eddie would always be there. He was a handsome kid."

"You couldn't tell that from what was left of him this morning," I said, not thinking.

"Oh, my God," she said, and reached for the Kleenex again. "He read a lot. His room in the apartment was lined with books. More books than I've ever read in my whole life. He had a hi-fi system and he was a rock music fan. Nora used to say she was going to have his room sound-proofed because it wasn't her kind of music. And Eddie was also a baseball nut. He'd watch games on TV, listen to them on radio, and now and then Nora would provide him with cash to go to Yankee Stadium or Shea. In his free time he played stickball down the block till it came out of his ears. Nora is what she is, but even the Reverend Martin would have to hand it to her for the way she raised her kid. He was a learner, headed for college, and a life as different from hers as anything you can imagine. God help her, Nora doesn't have anything to live for now."

I didn't mention that Dr. Morgan had suggested she might not have to face that.

"Do you have any idea at all why anyone would want to shoot the boy?"

"It's crazy," Linda said.

I suddenly had the first constructive idea I'd had in some hours. "I talked to one of his stickball friends, nice black kid named Norman," I said. "He told me Eddie lost the key to his apartment on Friday afternoon. He was going to have to get in by the fire escape. Could he have done that and found Nora involved with some guy who'd want to keep the boy from talking?''

Linda gave me a negative head shake. "No way," she said. "That apartment was Eddie's home. Nora would never have been playing games with anyone there. Eddie was free to come and go at any time. She'd never in the world have let him find out about the other side of her life."

"The Reverend Martin said he'd been there for supper one Sunday."

"With Eddie sitting across the table from him," Linda said. "It had to be that way or she wouldn't have had Martin there."

So much for positive thinking.

WHEN YOU'VE BEEN in trouble somewhere away from home, getting back to familiar surroundings has a way of making you feel safe and secure. The Beaumont might seem like a huge and impersonal place to you, glamor, glitter, even a kind of cold efficiency that is a little scary. To me it's home. It's also the place where I work. To me it's like a small town where the faces on the street are friendly and familiar, where there are landmarks everywhere I look, landmarks of past times, warm, funny, perhaps even exciting. I know every byway and side street. I can open any door and find only what I expect to find. I can pick up the phone, dial an extension, and the expected voice will answer. In that town, my town, I would never think to look back over my shoulder for someone who might be stalking me. I could walk in off the street out of a violence-torn city, out of a terror-ridden world, and feel suddenly safe. If I had unsolved problems Papa was only a flight of stairs away, or down the hallway if I was in my own apartment, with the answers to everything. There could even be, I told myself drily, a lollipop for me if I'd been a good boy. Chambrun was as quick to reward as he was to criticize.

That evening, when I got back from the violence in the Village, from the world of prostitutes, and "picture palaces," and criminal blackmail, devoid of all fundamental decency, the usual magic wasn't there. When I came out of the basement garage where I left the hotel car and into the lobby I felt, absurdly, that I must have taken a wrong turn. The lobby, the reception room of my "home," was crowded with strangers. They weren't the well-fed, well-heeled, well-dressed clientele that usually strolled through on a Saturday night looking for their particular pleasure in dining, or drinking, or being entertained in the Blue Lagoon, or a game of chess or backgammon in the Spartan Bar, or visiting a famous friend in an upstairs suite. These were street people, dressed for no occasion that could be expected here, hungry for something sensational. There were the recognizable members of the press, waiting for the next thing to happen. Tonight this wasn't a safe home. It had been invaded by bloodthirsty rubberneckers. After all, it wasn't a safe place. There had been two murders here in the space of a few hours, and a third violence, somehow connected with the first two, blocks away. I saw not only more than the usual number of our own

security people on duty, but a half-dozen men circulating through the crowd who had to be cops. Somehow cops don't wear their business suits like anyone
else in the world. They might as well wear their badges
pinned to the lapels of their jackets they are so obvious. Maybe it's the grim way they look at you, as
though you must almost certainly be the villain they're
after.

I looked around for Mike Maggio, the night bell
captain, who should be visible but wasn't. I glanced
over at the front desk to see who was on duty there,
but Karl Nevers, the clerk who should be in charge,
was obscured by a small army of people asking him
God knows what. Then I saw three of four reporters
headed my way and I made a quick move for the safety
of the front office. I picked up the phone and dialed
Chambrun's extension. A woman's voice that sounded
unfamiliar answered.

"Ruysdale?" I asked, knowing that it wasn't.

"I'm sitting in for Miss Ruysdale, can I help you?"
the voice asked, obviously someone from the secre-
tarial pool.

I told her who I was and that I wanted to locate
Chambrun.

"I believe he's up in his penthouse, Mr. Haskell."

I dialed that extension and got no answer. To hell
with this dislocated place, I told myself. I would go up
to my rooms, which are just down the hall from
Chambrun's office on the second floor. A drink, a
shower, and a change of clothes would make me feel
better. Somehow I felt a little gritty after the violence

on Jane Street, the wailing Hispanic woman in the emergency room at St. Vincent's, and the glimpse into the soiled world of Zachary Thompson. Maybe I could scrub off some of the pious double-talk I'd had from the Reverend Leonard Martin.

I stepped out of the office and found myself confronted by Eliot Stevens, my reporter friend from International.

"So?" he said.

I brought him up to date on Nora Sands.

"Is she going to make it?" he asked.

"Not hopeful," I said. "What the hell are all those creeps doing in the lobby?"

He shrugged. "Stan Nelson has to appear sometime," he said. "If you've heard the late radio or TV, or seen the evening papers, you'll know your anonymous friend has made him the living star of the show. You won't let me down when you know something solid?"

"A promise is a promise," I said. "I haven't been able to locate Chambrun so I don't know what's been cooking here. When I've washed off some of the day's grime and caught up with the Man, I'll be circulating again."

I decided to go out the back way and took the service elevator up to the second floor. I walked down the corridor to Chambrun's office. The girl sitting at Miss Ruysdale's desk was, I recalled, Betty Somebody-or-other. Chambrun could have told me her last name, where she'd gone to school, and who her boyfriend was! I left a message for him—that I was back, in my rooms, changing for the evening. Then I went back down the corridor to my room, took out my keys, and unlocked the door. It was dark inside and I reached for the light switch.

I never made it. Someone gave me a violent shove from behind, I felt a bomb explode in my head and excruciating pain. A Roman candle went off in front of my eyes. I thought I heard someone shouting. I thought it might be me. Then I was falling, down, down, to the bottom of the earth and into a black abyss.

PART THREE

ONE

OBVIOUSLY I GOT LUCKY in that moment or I wouldn't be telling this story now.

How much longer it was after that explosion inside my head I had no idea. I was suddenly aware of some unfamiliar odor of disinfectant. I tried opening my eyes and was instantly blinded by an intolerably bright light. I shut my eyes tight then.

"Well, at least there's still some life in him," a grouchy male voice said, standing very close to me.

I realized I was lying flat on my back on something that wasn't a feather bed. I reached out blindly, feeling for something familiar.

"His arms move," the grouchy voice said. "Now, if the stupid sonofabitch will open his eyes and keep them open he may realize where he is."

I opened my eyes a slit and kept them open. The light took the shape of a fluorescent tube. A gray head bent over me and I recognized the lined, unsmiling face of Doc Partridge, the Beaumont's house physician.

"So, I'm not a bad dream," he said. "You're in the Beaumont's First Aid Section. You ought to be dead but you're not. In case you're interested, you have a relatively mild concussion."

I said something that sounded like "Glub, Glub!" Then I smelled something far pleasanter than the disinfectant. It was a woman's perfume, and Betsy Ruysdale swam into view. One of her warm hands closed over one of mine.

"Mark dear, welcome home," she said.

"What *happened?*" I managed to say, quite clearly.

"That's what everyone wants to know," Ruysdale said. I suppose she's in her late thirties, with coppery red hair and a lush figure. As I think I've mentioned, the rumor is that she is more to Chambrun than his "executive assistant," which is her official title. That rumor was enough to keep the wolves around the Beaumont at a distance, a fact that in occasional fantasies I have regretted. She is a very nice lady. "You got very lucky, Mark."

"My head doesn't feel lucky," I said.

"If you hadn't been lucky your head might have looked like Tony Camargo's when that creep got through with him down in the garage," Doc Partridge said. He is a sour old curmudgeon, but as a doctor I'd have let him do brain surgery on me if it was required.

"You may owe your life, indirectly, to all those gawking sightseers who've invaded the hotel since morning," Ruysdale said. "They've refused to go away so Mr. Chambrun and Jerry Dodd set up a special patrol of security people to make sure invaders weren't seeping into places they had no business to be. You know Alec Watson?"

"One of Jerry's men," I said.

"You owe him, Luv," Ruysdale said. "He was assigned to cover the mezzanine and the second floor. He'd just come up to the second floor when he saw you getting out your keys at the door to your apartment. As you got the door open a man, someone, came out of the linen closet right next to your place, and attacked you from behind. Alec let out a shout, drew his gun, and came running. I guess that shout turned the attacker away from you."

"Or you'd have had it!" Doc Partridge said.

"He lashed back at Alec with whatever his weapon was, caught him right across the jaw and knocked him flat," Ruysdale said.

"Broke his jaw in three places," Doc Partridge said.

"The man ran down the hall. Alec, almost blinded by pain, took several shots at him, but he must have missed because they haven't found any traces of blood anywhere. Mr. Chambrun and Hardy assume you never saw him."

"Not a glimpse. But Alec—?"

"It was all so quick," Ruysdale said. "He came out of the linen room and pushed you into your dark apartment before Alec realized what was happening. Afterwards, lying on the floor, his jaw broken, he says he just fired at a blur."

"Where is Alec now?"

"In the hospital," the doctor said. "He'll be drinking his meals through a glass tube for the next month!"

"I gather I wasn't important enough to take to the hospital," I said.

Doc Partridge gave me a sour look. "You must be feeling better to make a stupid crack like that," he said. "Someone intended to kill you. Take you to a public facility like a hospital and if he wanted to try again he could make it. Here Chambrun's got you surrounded with a small army. He seems to think you're worth protecting."

"How long have I been here?" I asked.

Ruysdale glanced at the little jeweled watch on her left wrist. "Just after midnight," she said. "You've been here a little more than four hours."

The journey to wherever and back had taken time!

"When the doctor says so, they're moving you up to Pierre's penthouse. You'll be easier to guard there."

"I'd rather be in my place," I said.

"Until they know who and why, the penthouse level is the easiest to protect," Ruysdale said.

WHO OR WHY? I didn't have the remotest idea. But as I thought about it I thought I came up with a sensible answer. The hotel was full of freaks who didn't belong there. The technique was one you read about in the papers or hear on radio and TV day after day. Some character coming home to his or her apartment—usually some old lady—is pushed in from behind when she gets the door open, slugged, and the place robbed. So one of the goons from that crowd in the lobby had been floating around upstairs where he didn't belong. Hidden in the linen room, he'd seen me go down the hall to Chambrun's office. When I came back and started to let myself into my apartment he saw his chance, went through the attack-from-behind routine, and only Alec Watson's unexpected arrival had kept him from cleaning out my place. That's what came of letting the outside world into our private, well-ordered kingdom.

"No way," Chambrun said.

Doc Partridge and Miss Ruysdale had taken me in a wheelchair, surrounded by three of Jerry Dodd's men, up to Chambrun's penthouse on the roof. I was bedded down in one of the guest rooms and Ruysdale made a list of things I wanted from my apartment. In the middle of that Chambrun and Lieutenant Hardy arrived.

Chambrun's first words were to Doc Partridge. "How is he?"

"Thick skull," the doctor said.

Chambrun looked at me. "Feel up to talking, Mark?"

The expression in his deep-set eyes was reward enough for a rather big headache. He cared, really cared how I was.

"Except there is nothing to talk about," I said. "I never saw the sonofabitch." I gave him my theory about the routine mugging-from-behind.

That's when he said, "No way." He explained they'd been over the second floor, the stairways leading up and down from it, the elevators. He seemed certain Alec Watson's bullets had missed. It turned out he'd fired four shots and they'd found all four slugs embedded in the mouldings and the ceiling on the second floor. Four clean misses. Watson had been in agony and half stunned when he tried.

"This bastard knew exactly how to get away, where the back stair is. He knew he could wait for you in the linen room. We're up against someone, Mark, who knows this hotel well. He knew where your apartment is, knew where to hide while he waited for you to show. He knew what Tony Camargo's routines were and where he could wait for him and bring him down."

I felt my eyes grow wide. "You think it's the same—?"

"I don't believe in coincidences, Mark. This man knows the hotel well enough to know where he could find keys to the Health Club and when they might be unguarded long enough for him to make an impression from them. He knows our routines, where things are, like your apartment, where things are kept, like the wrecking bar he used to beat Tony to death on the loading platform. One thing he didn't know and it may have saved your life, Mark."

"That being—?"

"He didn't know that we'd set up a security patrol on the mezzanine and the second floor to keep those creeps in the lobby from drifting upstairs."

"We have to believe it's someone who knows the hotel inside out," Hardy said. "Probably someone working here."

"If it is," Chambrun said in a tight, hard voice, "I will take personal pleasure in shoving him off this roof, which is a forty-story drop!"

"But why me?" I asked.

"The same reason that he wiped out Tony Camargo," Chambrun said. "You know something that would attach him to the murder of Eddie Sands. Tony knew that something, but it hadn't clicked yet. You better get it to click with you, Mark, or it won't be safe for you to walk out of this place!" He stared at me. "So think, man, think!"

My mind was as blank as a freshly scrubbed blackboard.

"We seem to be living in a world of slow takes," Chambrun said. He sounded impatient. "You can't remember something, but a killer thinks you may and you become a target. Tony Camargo hadn't remembered something, but the killer was sure he would. It's easy to think Nora Sands may be a member of the club—would remember something sooner or later and had to be silenced."

"And the boy in the pool?" Hardy asked.

"Would remember, or had remembered and was ready to talk," Chambrun suggested.

"It doesn't add up, Pierre," Hardy said, scowling. "These people all operate or operated in different worlds. Mark and Tony Camargo never heard of the Sandses till after the boy was murdered. The Sands woman and her son have no connection with the hotel."

"Wake up, Walter," Chambrun said. "There is a connection and he's just across the roof. Stan Nelson!"

I must have been a lot woozier than I realized at the time because I have no memory of the ending of that conversation or Chambrun and Hardy leaving me. I must have dozed off trying to make something "click" in my head that wasn't there. When I opened my eyes again the sun was streaming through the bedroom windows and it was another day. Sunday, and for no sensible reason I wondered where the Reverend Leonard Martin took his message on the Lord's Day.

I smelled coffee and it was tempting. I reached up and touched the back of my head. Doc Partridge had left some kind of medical patch or pad there. I wasn't tempted to press hard to see how it felt.

"So, you're alive," a voice said from the doorway.

If I tell you that I have a kind of a crush on the lady who was standing there you might be inclined to laugh. Victoria Haven admits, without blushing, that she was born in the year 1900. She is tall, stands very straight, and has a mass of henna-colored hair, a shade that God never dreamed of. There are wrinkles in her face, but the high cheekbones, the wide mouth, the bright blue eyes are remnants of great beauty. Thirty-five or forty years ago when parts of the Beaumont were co-op apartments she had bought the middle penthouse on the roof and lived there ever since. "With my Japanese friend," she would tell anyone who asked. Her "Japanese friend" was a hostile little Japanese spaniel who had no use for anyone but his elegant mistress. His name was Toto. In my time there have been two Totos and I've been told there was a third one before I came to work for Chambrun. Mrs.

Haven has some kind of pull with the Man, because pets are strictly against the rules of the hotel. There were even rumors that years ago there had been some kind of young man–older woman relationship between Mrs. Haven and Chambrun. Whatever there was in the past, Mrs. Haven was permitted to violate the no-pet rule. She not only kept him up there on the roof, but every afternoon about five o'clock Toto accompanied his mistress down to the Trapeze Bar on the mezzanine where she had a corner table reserved. Toto sat on his own red satin cushion on a chair beside her while she held court. Men of all ages seemed to flock to her table, and in spite of her age she was still capable of enchantment. She wears so much gaudy jewelry that the manager of Tiffany's, seeing her, must have been tempted to run back to his store to check out his inventory.

"Every one of these things," she told me one day, "is a memento of a romance. And when I say romance, Haskell, you should visualize a capital R."

"When she was a young girl," Chambrun told me, "she was a dancer in a Broadway cabaret, toast of the town. She had legs that would have made Betty Grable, her ancestors and descendants, envious. They broke the mold when Victoria was invented." He said it with genuine affection.

"Are you the coffee maker?" I asked her.

She gave me her still brilliant smile. "Smell good?"

"Marvelous!"

"Have you tried walking yet?"

"No."

"So toddle off to the little boys' room and do your morning whatevers. I'll have an egg and toast as well for you." She started to go and turned back. "If you fall down I shan't be too upset. I'll have to call on that handsome young man in number three to pick you up."

"Handsome young man?"

"Stan Nelson," she said. "Can you imagine having him for a neighbor? I've been swooning over his singing for the last twenty years."

I grinned at her. "Make it two eggs and I'll introduce you to Stan after breakfast," I said.

"My dear Haskell, for that I'll add a few strips of bacon," she said, and was gone.

Dear Betsy Ruysdale had produced all the things I'd wanted from my place. I shaved, and since Doc Partridge hadn't told me not to get the patch on my head wet, I showered. I wasn't going anywhere so I put on a clean pair of pajamas and a white terry-cloth robe and joined the cook.

As I stepped out of my temporary bedroom I was greeted by a snarl, small but menacing. Toto, snuffling through his snub nose, imagined he was in charge no matter where he happened to be.

"Knock it off, Buster," I told him.

He appeared to be measuring me for the kill.

"Toto!" Mrs. Haven called from the kitchen.

The little bully recognized real authority. He gave me a "get-you-later" look and waddled off to join Mrs. Haven. I glanced at Chambrun's beautiful gold

French clock on the mantel. It was a quarter past one in the afternoon! I had slept right around the clock.

I guess that knowledge brought me back to earth. I walked over to a side table and switched on the radio to CBS, which does a perpetual news show. They were talking about violence in the Middle East. Mrs. Haven appeared in the kitchen doorway, an apron tied around her still shapely waist.

"The Sands woman is still fighting to make it," she told me.

I switched off the radio. Mrs. Haven had obviously been staying abreast of things.

"Has she been able to talk?" I asked.

"No, and they're not hopeful," she said. "Your breakfast is ready."

She'd set up a place for me in the little alcove in Chambrun's kitchen. As she'd promised there was juice, bacon and boiled eggs, toast, and coffee. I sat down, but I suddenly wasn't very hungry. However far out Nora Sands' lifestyle might be, she had seemed so very alive, so vital in my brief contact with her.

"Which Pierre thinks should make you take your situation seriously," Mrs. Haven said. "He thinks the same animal who attacked you, Haskell, used the same technique on Nora Sands. She went home from here, in shock over what she found here at the Beaumont, went to open her apartment, was shoved in from behind, beaten unconscious—and then this monster took his time tearing up her apartment, looking for something he either did or didn't find.

You'd better open your eggs, Haskell. They won't be worth eating presently.''

"Did or didn't find?" I asked, cracking open a boiled egg that was done just perfectly for my taste.

"They have no way of knowing," Mrs. Haven said. "The people who lived in the apartment can't tell them what's missing, if anything. The boy is dead, Nora Sands is flirting with death."

The coffee was perfect, the bacon crisp perfection.

"I didn't dream you could cook," I said.

She gave me a broad smile. "Basic training," she said. "The way to a man's heart . . ."

I couldn't concentrate on the food, perfect as it was. "None of it fits together for me," I said. "We haven't the faintest idea why Eddie Sands was shot. I found out he'd lost his apartment key and was planning to get in by going up the fire escape. Maybe he caught someone searching the place."

"That had to be Friday afternoon or early evening," Mrs. Haven said. "A whole day before poor Tony Camargo was attacked, more than that before his mother got here, you even later. I know Pierre thinks the order in which it happened is important."

"Order?"

"The boy first. That was the start, the beginning. The boy saw something, knew something, that was a danger to someone. Where was he killed? It's hard to imagine that it was anywhere else but here in the hotel. You don't travel around the streets of New York carrying a body! Though God knows there's enough violence to make a dead man pretty commonplace.

You know how old I am, Haskell. Nineteen-hundred was the historic year of my birth!'' She laughed. ''I used to walk the streets of this city at two, three, four o'clock in the morning. I was a show girl, furs, jewels. I felt as safe on the streets as I had on my grandmother's back porch in Dorset, Vermont. We never locked a door in those days, never had any fear of people. Today I can't walk down Fifth Avenue in broad daylight without being afraid someone will snatch at a necklace I'm wearing, or an earring, or my purse. If I get shoved under the wheels of a taxi it will just be another everyday event. Do you know I haven't been outside the hotel since they passed a law that I had to go around after Toto with a shovel and a plastic bag to pick up his leavings? When I had to be that undignified I decided I might as well stay where I was safe. I'm a little too old to learn karate.''

''Which gets us where?'' I asked, breaking off a piece of toast into my eggs.

''This animal, this killer, is a part of today's world,'' she said. ''It's a world I really regret I've lived to see, Haskell. Drugs, cheap sex, violence for the fun of it, no value on life itself. A crazy kid tried to kill the president to impress an actress he's never met; John Lennon shot in his tracks by someone who's never even met him; the Pope a target for a mad terrorist who had no personal reason for his crime. Now we have a fifteen-year-old whose own mother doesn't know who his father is! Then Tony Camargo, who chatted casually with McPherson five minutes before he's beaten to death, apparently had nothing on his mind; then Nora Sands, who can't tell anyone why she was brutalized and has no friend who can guess at why; and finally you, Haskell! You are the only one who can talk and who still has all his wits—and you don't know what to tell anyone.''

"There isn't anything to tell," I said. "It's just a coincidence. Someone in that crowd that was milling around the lobby decided he could find something worth stealing in this place. He got to the second floor, saw me going into my place, and used what is now a common street violence to take whatever I might have worth anything.''

"Please, please, my dear Haskell, don't be an ass!" Mrs. Haven said. "If you can't come up with whatever it is someone thinks you know they'll be holding a funeral for you. God knows it isn't even safe to die today, with vandals ripping up our graveyards.''

She was serious, and she wasn't an idiot. I reached for my coffee cup. It was a warm spring day but I felt a chill run along my spine. Was there something I'd managed to black out? The only person I'd known before all had started with the dead boy in the pool was Tony Camargo, and he was just somebody I said hello to when we passed on our jobs. We hadn't been friends, just acquaintances. I didn't know anything about anyone, or any fact relating to all this, that could possibly be dangerous to anyone. Or did I?

The phone rang and Toto expressed his resentment from the corner to which he'd retreated.

"That will be Pierre to find out if you've surfaced," Mrs. Haven said. "The switchboard was ordered to protect you from anything casual.'' She picked up the phone. ''Yes, Pierre?'' She listened for a moment and then she said, ''Oh my God! Yes, I'll tell him.'' She put the receiver back in place and faced me. ''Nora Sands died a half an hour ago—without talking.''

I found myself standing up.

''Pierre's coming,'' Mrs. Haven said. ''Haskell, you've *got* to remember what it is you've blotted out. You'll be next, you know, if you don't!''

I SUSPECT ALL OF US ARE brought up to accept the fact that we are constantly surrounded by danger. All of childhood is surrounded by warnings. "It's raining, Mark. If you don't wear your rubbers you'll catch cold. Look both ways before you cross the street—or else. Don't talk to strangers—it may be a burglar trying to find out when the family won't be at home." I could give you a list as long as my arm. My mother saw disaster everywhere. My father, on the other hand, was a fatalist. "You slip on the soap in the bathtub and break your neck. If your number is up, it's up."

In today's world, as Victoria Haven had just been pointing out, the dangers are very real. In any fifteen-minute newscast on radio or TV you are certain to hear of at least three or four violences—a holdup-robbery-murder sequence, or hijacking and hostage taking, a fire in which people die is of "suspicious origin." Rape, sodomy, God knows what other aberrations, are everywhere. But I know I don't walk around every day expecting to be the target of some horror. I take it for granted it will happen to some other guy, some other group, people I don't know. I've been confronted with violence and death in Chambrun City. Security is better in the Beaumont than in most "cities," but when violence does take place it has never involved friends, people I know well. My face has never, until that Sunday, been in the center of the bulls-eye.

It isn't a pleasant sensation, I can tell you. I didn't quite believe it yet, but I couldn't ignore the possibility. Chambrun, Hardy, Jerry Dodd, and my remarkable old lady friend, who had more experience with life than any of us, were all convinced that what had happened to me was directly connected with two murders—three now, for God sake.

"You think I've inconveniently forgotten something," I said to Chambrun when he and Jerry Dodd appeared in the penthouse. Chambrun looked fresh and rested, but I guessed it was a surface accomplishment. There was dark trouble in his deep-set eyes. It was comforting to know that he was concerned for his beloved hotel and for its population for whom he felt responsible. "I keep telling myself it's not so, Boss, because I can't imagine where to start trying to remember."

We had moved out onto the terrace outside the penthouse, shielded from the afternoon sun by a wide green awning. Chambrun sat sunk in a white wicker armchair, eyes squinted against the smoke from one of his flat-shaped Egyptian cigarettes. Jerry Dodd paced restlessly up and down by the row of flower boxes, looking out over the roof at Mrs. Haven's penthouse and the one that housed Stan Nelson and his two people. Mrs. Haven brought a tray of fresh coffee in mugs.

"Don't get to like this service, Pierre," she said. "I'm not about to turn housemaid."

He gave her a sort of faraway smile. "I've always hoped that you might someday be my slave, Victoria. Let me go on dreaming." He turned his attention to me. "There are several areas you may have to cover, Mark, but it begins here at the hotel. I'm personally convinced that when you go back over the last forty-eight hours here in the hotel you may suddenly remember what a psychotic killer so urgently wants you to forget."

"Until Carl Hulman found the Sands boy in the pool yesterday morning everything here had been routine," I said.

"Oh, come on, Mark, get your head screwed on," he said. "Just because it hasn't been routine is why you could forget something which at the time seemed unimportant."

"But I tell you—"

"Let me tell you, since you don't seem to be making sense," he said. "Let's go back to Thursday noon. Thursday noon Stan Nelson, his bodyguard and his musical genius, checked in. You took them up to their suite, made sure that everything was arranged for them as Nelson wanted it."

"I've done that five or six times in the last five or six years," I said. "And for hundreds of other famous guests since I've been working here. Routine."

"Of course it's routine," he said, impatient with me. "The minute Stan Nelson walked into this hotel nothing has been quite normal again. A thousand people who had never been in this hotel before—unless it was at Nelson's last telethon—inundated us like a hurricane's high tide. Security had to be heightened. Not routine. The comings and goings of our guests, our regular clientele, were interrupted, dislocated. Not routine. Starting early in the evening, intensifying at midnight when the telethon started, you were constantly in and out of the ballroom, ignoring your usual patterns. Not routine. For twenty-four hours that unusual pattern for you persisted. Not routine. Then, yesterday morning, Hulman found the dead boy in the pool and Mr. Anonymous began informing the world and pointing at Stan Nelson. You have none of your regular jobs since then; you've been out into the world of stickball, of professional pornography, of the New Morality. Routine? Come on, Mark, come on!''

In a way he was right, of course. The whole telethon time in the hotel wasn't an everyday occurrence. But my job was to deal with out-of-the-ordinary situations. In that sense it was routine. I had done it before and in dozens of other excitements created by the presence in the Beaumont of famous and glamorous people. But the deaths of the last two days?

I had been at the front desk at noon on Thursday when Stan Nelson, Johnny Floyd, and Butch Mancuso arrived. I was waiting for them because Johnny had phoned from Kennedy Airport that they were on their way. I ferried Stan and his bodyguard directly up to the suite on the thirty-fifth floor. Johnny Floyd stayed behind to do the formal registering for all three of them at the front desk. We managed all that without raising any squeals of delight and surprise in the lobby. Stan had gone unrecognized. Nothing to remember there.

Up in the suite Stan had given me a typed list, prepared in advance, of things he wanted done in the ballroom—the position of the microphones and speakers, the piano, exactly what he wanted in the private rest room he would have to use during a twenty-four-hour nonstop musical marathon. I didn't need the list. I had done it all for him at least four times before. Nothing out of the ordinary here.

Stan ordered a substantial meal for all three of them to be brought up from room service. After they'd eaten they would all go to bed and try to get an extra quota of sleep until they had to get up and dress for the midnight beginning of the telethon. The switchboard was to be informed that no calls be put through until they got different instructions. If anyone claimed it was an emergency the call was to be put through to me and I would make the decision.

"And it better not be anything except that the hotel is on fire," Johnny Floyd told me.

All quite usual.

There was a breakfast order to be put in for eleven o'clock that night. I, personally, was to put through a call to wake them at ten-thirty. Jerry Dodd's people were to cover the front corridor outside the suite and in the service area at the rear so that no eager Nelson fan could come pounding on the doors, front or back, during the rest period.

I had arranged all that before, could have done it in my sleep. Routine!

"So let's pick it up at ten-thirty," Chambrun said.

"The first thing that wasn't routine happened about four in the afternoon on Thursday," I said. "I took a nap myself. It was going to be a long night. I dreamed about a girl—but never mind that. It's private and had nothing to do with Stan Nelson."

"Oh, dear," Mrs. Haven said. "I thought you were going to get interesting at last, Haskell."

"Ten-thirty," Chambrun said, hiding any irritation he felt.

"I had dressed for the evening—dinner jacket," I said. "I called Nelson's suite and Johnny Floyd answered. I checked with room service to make sure their 'breakfast' was on the fire. Then I went downstairs to check out on the ballroom. A foretaste of the future was already on hand."

Chambrun nodded. "People," he said.

"Crowded into the lobby and in the corridor outside the ballroom. Out onto the street, I think. Mass insanity, but routine for the telethon. I had to go into the ballroom from the back way, or risk being trampled to death."

"Nothing unusual? You didn't stop to talk to anyone you hadn't expected to see?"

"No. The sound technicians were in place in the ballroom, mikes where they should be, speakers where they should be. Outside the closed door you could hear those crazy chicks, squealing and giggling. It would have made you sick if you didn't stop to realize each one of them was prepared to make a contribution to a worthy cause. You can't get into the ballroom unless you make a contribution or a pledge."

"Then?"

"Nothing, until Stan and Johnny and Butch Mancuso turned up at a quarter to twelve, using the service elevator to get down there."

"They report any problems or difficulties?"

"No. Everything smooth as silk. You know how the telethon begins? Johnny sits down at the piano, plays a brief intro, and then Stan begins to sing 'Oh What a Beautiful Morning' from *Oklahoma*. The doors are opened and the screeching mob shoves its way in. After that it's bedlam for twenty-four hours, except when Stan sings, which is about every twenty minutes. How he lives through that I'll never know."

"So the mob is in," Chambrun said. "Did you see anything unusual, anyone behaving in a peculiar fashion?"

"Everybody behaves peculiarly at those telethons. They go quietly mad for twenty-four hours."

Chambrun's mouth was a thin, tight line. "Someone went not so quietly mad," he said. "Three people dead and a fourth under fire! Think, Mark! Someone shouting threats over the din? Someone giving Security a bad time?"

"I'd seen it all before," I said.

Chambrun twisted impatiently in his chair. He was fishing in a pool where there were no fish. At least I couldn't stir one up. Projecting ahead, through the early hours of that Friday morning, all through a day in which every normal procedure in the hotel was off its tracks, into the evening and up to the finish at midnight—twenty-four hours of madhouse—I still couldn't come up with a single memorable moment. There had been other telethons where funny things happened, like the time when some dizzy doll stood up on a chair in the ballroom and let her dress drop, leaving her stark naked while Stan sang "You're Delightful, You're Delovely—" The screams and shouts shook the chandeliers in the distant lobby. Good clean fun in the name of cancer research. There was the time when a girl fell off the balcony that surrounds the ballroom right into the center of a cut-glass bowl of wine punch and sat there, soaked from head to foot, applauding as Stan sang "Ain't She Sweet."

"The only thing that was unusual about Friday's telethon," I told Chambrun, "is that nothing unusual happened."

"Except that a killer was on the prowl," he said.

Victoria Haven interrupted us. "Oh my, here comes my big moment," she said.

I looked out across the roof and saw Stan Nelson and his two guys headed our way.

They came straight to where we were sitting. Stan, wearing a white linen jacket, a navy-blue shirt open at the neck, was his handsome self except that his usual friendly smile was missing. Johnny Floyd and Butch Mancuso in summer suits were right out of an old Warner Brothers gangster film.

"I'm sorry to interrupt, Mr. Chambrun," Stan said, "but I just heard the news on the radio."

Chambrun introduced the three men to Mrs. Haven. Stan gave her a polite but disinterested little nod. Toto took the stage for a few minutes, giving the three men a sort of group snarl. Mancuso, the gunman, took a startled step backwards.

"Toto!" Mrs. Haven said, and the little spaniel retreated back under a chair. "Toto has never heard you sing, Mr. Nelson." The old lady gave Stan her brightest smile. "If he had, he would have welcomed you."

"Nora Sands is dead," Stan said to Chambrun, ignoring Mrs. Haven.

"I know," Chambrun said.

"I've been trying to reach Lieutenant Hardy on the phone," Stan said. "I want Johnny to go down to where she is to see if there is anything we can do. We agreed none of us would leave the hotel without the lieutenant's okay, but no one seems to know where he is."

"What do you mean 'do'?" Chambrun asked.

"She has no family, with the boy gone," Stan said. "And there they are, both of them, needing to be buried, to have done for them whatever one has to have done."

"She has Zachary Thompson," Chambrun said. "Mark tells me he was at St. Vincent's, preparing to pay Miss Sands' medical bills."

"She was alive then," Johnny Floyd said in his rasping voice, cigarette bobbing up and down between his lips. "Dead, whatever she had on him is dead, too. He doesn't have to help her now."

"Had on him?" Chambrun asked.

"She worked for him—eighteen, twenty years," Johnny said. "In that time she must have collected quite a lot on him. He'd pay to keep that quiet. Sonofabitch runs a kind of blackmail factory. Now that Nora's gone he couldn't care less what happens to—to what's left." Always angry Johnny.

"If she had so much on him how did it happen she came to you for help?" Chambrun asked. "You told us yesterday you'd helped her out from time to time, with Mr. Nelson's money."

"Not many people understood Nora," Stan said. He put his hand on Johnny's shoulder as if to reassure him. "She had an extraordinary code of fair play. Whatever she had on Thompson she wouldn't use it to force him to help. He'd stood by her once when she was in trouble. She could have made trouble for me and my marriage by claiming I was the boy's father. She didn't, because she wasn't sure it was a fact."

"But she went to Floyd for help," Chambrun said. "That was a way of putting the heat on you, wasn't it?"

"Johnny may have thought that. I don't," Stan said. "Johnny has been a part of my life forever—before Nora, and specially during the two years Nora *was* my life. She needed help because of the boy. She would have crawled on her hands and knees to an old friend like Johnny if she needed something for the boy. I'm certain she wasn't trying to burn me. In any event, I don't want some poverty burial for her and the boy. I want a decent service for them and someone to say good-bye to her in the proper way. I owe her that for two rather special years she gave me."

"Some special!" Johnny said. "In the hay with anyone who came along!"

Stan gave his friend a tired smile. "You smoke too many cigarettes, Johnny. You'll probably die of lung cancer, but you can't stop. Nora couldn't stop. She couldn't break a habit she'd contracted long before I came on the scene."

Chambrun wasn't interested in Nora's sex life. "You told us yesterday, Floyd, that you'd been helping Miss Sands. You had her address and telephone number. When did all this start, helping her to protect Stan?"

"At the telethon two years ago," Johnny said. "She called me here at the hotel, asked if I'd see her. I told her I'd meet her away from here. I didn't want to risk her running into Stan. It would have been embarrassing and painful for him."

"So you went to her apartment."

"No. I never went to her apartment. We met in the old Roosevelt Bar on Madison Avenue. The kid had to have some kind of a tonsil operation. She was flat. I loaned her the money. She gave me her address and phone number and I gave her a way to reach me in California. She did, twice after that. There'd been some kind of complication following the boy's operation. He had to be hospitalized for a spell. I helped out those two times. Since then, nothing. I thought I'd hear from her during the telethon a year ago, and this time. Nothing. I thought I was being set up to be a permanent sucker. She didn't play it that way."

"It wouldn't have been Nora's style," Stan said.

"You told us yesterday you never saw the boy," Chambrun said, keeping at Johnny.

"Never. I only saw Nora once—I mean since the old days—that time in the Roosevelt Bar. The other two times she asked for help was by long distance to California."

"You didn't see the boy at the telethon Friday night?"

"I wouldn't have known him if he was there," Johnny said. "If he was resurrected and he walked in here right now I wouldn't know if it was him."

"I know you couldn't tell anything by what was left of his face down there in the pool," Chambrun said. "But if we had a picture of him do you think you might know whether you'd seen him Friday night or not?"

"For Christ sake, Mr. Chambrun, we go all kinds of places, all around the world, night clubs, theaters, outdoor concerts. We see, I guess, hundreds of thousands of faces. I'd have to have a reason to notice, like someone had two heads, or an ugly scar, or someone dropped a drunk on my foot!"

"Whoever killed Miss Sands tore her place to pieces," Chambrun said. "Sergeant Keller, in charge down there, tells us there were no pictures. You'd think a woman who was so fond of a child as Miss Sands appears to have been, would have had pictures of him. Papers, Keller tells us, were burned in the fireplace. Perhaps—"

I had a bright idea. "There's a girl who was a close friend of Nora's who came to St. Vincent's with Thompson. She works at the Private Lives Club. Linda. They don't have last names. Would Nora have had a picture of the boy in her dressing room at the club? Linda would know, I think."

Chambrun gave me a bitter look. "It's too bad you can't think as clearly as that about something you may need to remember to save your life," he said.

THE PRIVATE LIVES CLUB was closed on Sundays. I should have remembered that, among other things. Linda had mentioned spending time on their day off with Nora. Not knowing Linda's last name there was no way of looking her up in the phone book, in case she had a phone. The club drew a perpetual busy signal. Zach Thompson had an unlisted phone which Lieutenant Hardy was able to pry out of the telephone company. No answer when it was called. Dr. Morgan, when St. Vincent's was called, was in surgery. He might have been helpful.

I had imagined Chambrun might have sent me to hunt for Linda but he had grimmer plans for me. Until I could unearth whatever it was that had made me a target for a killer I was not to leave the hotel rooftop.

"Here you are at least safe for now," Chambrun said. "A cop and one of our security men are guarding the fire stairs. A cop is riding the one elevator that comes up here. No one is going to get above the thirty-ninth floor without being checked out down to his bare skin. So sit somewhere and think! Think about every minute of every hour from the time Stan Nelson and Company checked in here on Thursday until you walked into your apartment last night and got slugged. Write it down, go over it. Somewhere there is something, Mark, and you damn well need to find it!"

And so in the end I installed myself at Chambrun's desk in the living room, equipped with a legal pad and a couple of ball points, and tried to go back into what appeared to be a fog of inconsequential nothings.

Things happened in the next couple of hours that I learned about later. What didn't happen was a recall of anything that might make me dangerous to a psychotic killer.

While I stewed away at my memory exercise Lieutenant Hardy sent one of his Homicide boys down to the Private Lives Club in the Village. He figured that even though nobody answered the phone down there someone must be on the scene, a watchman, a maintenance man. He came closer than that to striking oil. Some sort of janitor character answered a determined ringing at the front door, but when Sergeant Lawson identified himself as a cop, Zach Thompson himself emerged from his private office.

"I suppose I should have expected you," he said to Sergeant Lawson.

"Nobody answered the phone here," Lawson said.

"We're not open on Sundays," Thompson said. "Every newsman in New York has been after me since Nora was attacked."

"You know that she's dead?"

"Of course I know. What do you think this is, some kind of desert island? The goddamn story goes round and round on the radio. What do you want of me, Lawson?"

"I was sent here for a specific purpose," Lawson said. "But as long as you're here there are some questions."

"What specific purpose?"

"We're looking for a picture of Eddie Sands," Lawson told him. "We hope to find someone who may have seen him at the Beaumont. The body is so disfigured from the wound there's no way anyone could tell whether they'd seen him alive or not."

"You thought I might have a picture?" Thompson found that amusing.

"We thought Miss Sands might have had one in her dressing room."

"Let's look," Thompson said.

He took Lawson through the elaborate bar and lounge which was the centerpiece of the club to a backstage area. It seemed that all of the girls dressed in one large space with adjoining showers and bathrooms. Nora had had a private room of her own. There was a dressing table with makeup lights surrounding a mirror; a couple of comfortable upholstered armchairs, a small cot or a bed on which she could rest if she chose.

The top of the dressing table was bare. Thompson frowned at it.

"Looks as if someone cleaned it out," he said. "There should be jars and bottles, comb and brush, tissues, stuff like that. There were the few times I saw it.'' There were drawers on either side of the dressing table. He opened them. They were empty.

"There are clothes in the closet,'' Lawson said.

"The wardrobe belongs to the club, to me,'' Thompson said.

"Mark Haskell, back at the hotel, mentioned meeting a girl who was Miss Sands' friend, at St. Vincent's. Someone named Linda.''

"Of course!'' Thompson said. "Linda probably took her personal things for safekeeping. Once the word was out this place could become a den of thieves. Nora wouldn't need her perfumes and creams and the stage jewelry she wore. The other broads who work here would probably have cleaned her out. I've got a phone number for Linda in my office, let's try.''

Lawson told me later he thought Thompson looked like a character out of a horror film, with his Fu Manchu mustache and his beard, and the white smile that reflected no humor.

Thompson's office embarrassed Lawson. The walls were decorated with blown-up color photographs of naked girls in suggestive poses, center-fold girls. Lawson felt he shouldn't be looking at them but he couldn't help himself.

Thompson read his mind and laughed. "Some of the best white meat that's worked for me over the years,'' he said. He found a telephone number in a card index file on his desk and dialed a number. "Linda?... Zach Thompson here.... Yes, I know.... Well, of course it's awful.... Look, luv, there's a cop here looking for a photograph of Eddie Sands. They thought Nora might have had one in her dressing room. Someone's cleaned out her personal things and I thought it might be you.... Oh, good.... Is there a picture?... Well, can you trot over here with it?... Yes, we'll wait." He put down the phone. "Like we thought, Linda took her things, and there is a picture. She's bringing it."

"Her last name?" Lawson asked.

Thompson grinned at him. "We don't give out last names to customers. It's a kind of life insurance. But in your case..." He shrugged. "Linda Zazkowski. Polish, I imagine."

Lawson wrote it down in his notebook. "Address and phone number."

"She can give you that if she wants to," Thompson said. "I protect my people."

"Not Nora Sands," Lawson said, slipping the notebook back in his pocket.

"Look, Sergeant, I've got over two hundred girls working for me across the country, plus bartenders, and musicians, and waiters, and cooks, and cleaning people, and office help, and a whole magazine staff, and God knows what else. It would take an army to protect each one of them every minute of the time. I don't dig into their private lives unless it has some bearing on my business."

"But you knew Nora Sands well. I understand she's worked for you a long time."

Thompson's face darkened. "She was special," he said. "Most of my girls work for me for two, three years. They're burned out at twenty-two or three, or they hook some rich john to take care of them. Nora was different. She got better with age. And she became a first-class manager. I could leave her to run this club for months at a time, if I had to cover my other places. Yes, I knew her well, and trusted her, which is more than I can say for most people who work for me.''

''She made enemies?''

''Until yesterday I'd have said 'No way.'''

''But now you think—''

''If it hadn't been for the boy I'd have said it was just a vicious break-in and robbery,'' Thompson said. ''The two things have to be connected. I go along with that wise guy up at the Beaumont, Pierre Chambrun. I don't believe in coincidences.''

''So you have a theory?''

Thompson's eyes narrowed. ''You have to have evidence if you don't want to get sued out of all your assets,'' he said

''Just between us,'' Lawson said casually.

''You know some of Nora's history,'' Thompson said. ''It's right under your nose up there at the Beaumont.''

''Meaning Stan Nelson?''

''What else?'' Thompson said. The mention of Stan Nelson seemed to stir up some kind of anger in the man, Lawson said. ''He was Nora's one big hunk of living outside of my orbit.''

''He wants to pay for the funerals,'' Lawson said.

"Why not? That'll make him look real good, won't it?"

"In whose eyes?" Lawson asked. "Stan Nelson doesn't need anything to improve his public image."

"Maybe in your eyes," Thompson said, his smile twisted. "Sooner or later, unless you've lost all your marbles, you cops are going to have to start thinking about Mr. Nice Guy."

"Why?"

"What's the matter with you, Sergeant? You keep asking kindergarten questions."

I realize I haven't described Sergeant Lawson. I guess if I were to say that all Chinese look alike you'd call me a racist. Well, to me all cops look alike, except those who are working undercover and take on a variety of disguises. Lawson is about six feet, athletic build, short sandy hair cut 1940s style. He has the perpetual look of the officer who pokes his head in the window of your car and says, "Let me see your license, please." Cool, impersonal, reacting outwardly to nothing you say, nothing mirrored in pale blue eyes. If Thompson thought he could jolt Lawson out of his cool he'd picked the wrong man.

"Why should we be thinking about Stan Nelson?" Lawson asked again.

"Because Nora Sands was beaten to a pulp by someone who had to keep her quiet," Thompson said. "Nelson was a big number in her life. Someone searching for something she had on him."

"Years ago," Lawson said. "And we know exactly where Nelson was when Nora Sands was attacked. He was in the Beaumont, under protection and surveillance."

"He could afford to hire someone to do his dirty work," Thompson said. "He's so rich it hurts to think about it."

"Did you think of that yourself," Lawson asked, "or did you hear on the radio what our Mr. Anonymous told us?"

"So I heard it on the radio, but I also thought of it myself," Thompson said. "You didn't buy the garbage Johnny Floyd dished out to you up there in the Health Club, did you? He helped Nora out to keep her from messing up Stan Nelson's life? Helped her out with Nelson's money? Oh, brother!"

"So how do you figure it?" Lawson asked.

"She had something on Nelson. They had to buy her off. This time around she went too far."

"Are you suggesting Miss Sands was a blackmailer?" Lawson asked.

"Not as a business," Thompson said, "but if she needed something for that kid of hers she'd bring any pressure to bear she could to get help."

"You were a much older and longer friend of hers than Nelson," Lawson said. "Why wouldn't she come to you for help if she needed it? You'd stood by her before, hadn't you—a lawsuit out in California? Anyway, having worked for you for years she must have had enough on you to send you up for the rest of your natural life."

"I don't have to take that kind of crap from you, Lawson!" Thompson exploded.

"When I charge you with something I'll read you your rights," Lawson said. "All I'm saying is the same shoe fits different feet."

"Screw you!" Thompson said.

"Why would somebody's hit man kill the boy?" Lawson asked, as though nothing had interrupted their original line of talk.

"More guessing games?" Thompson said.

"At this point guesses are all we've got to go on," Lawson said. "Try one on me."

Lawson told us afterwards that Thompson seemed to make a considerable effort to control his anger. He made a kind of grinding sound with his teeth before he spoke.

"So I'll make a guess for you," he said. "But mind you, that's what it is, a guess." He took a deep breath. "That was Friday night. The boy played stickball late. Nora had already come here to work when he got home. My guess is that he found someone in the apartment, probably searching for something— something Nora had on Nelson. The boy tried to run and they shot him."

"There in the apartment?"

Thompson shrugged. "Maybe not. Maybe they grabbed him, took him up to the Beaumont to question him there, found out he knew too much, shot him and dumped him in the pool."

"You do know that Nelson, Floyd, and the bodyguard Mancuso were all in the ballroom at the hotel, in the middle of the telethon? Airtight alibis for all three!"

"The hit man took the kid up there, got his instructions, and carried them out. He'd have had no difficulty getting into the ballroom to talk to one or all of them."

"When Miss Sands came up to the hotel on Saturday morning to identify her son she didn't say anything about her apartment being entered or searched or robbed," Lawson said.

"Look, Sergeant, I don't have to tell you, a cop, that break-in and robberies aren't unheard of in this neck of the woods. People in this neighborhood would know her habits. If nothing important was missing she wouldn't have had it on her mind looking down at that dead kid with a hole in his face!"

"Wouldn't connect it with what happened to the boy?"

"He'd apparently been killed in the hotel! He had Stan Nelson's autograph in his pocket!"

"And the hit man was waiting for her when she got home. This time there was no doubt about a search."

"When the kid was connected with her," Thompson said, "they couldn't wait. They had to find whatever she had on them, and fast. They tried to beat her first, to get her to tell them where what they wanted was kept. When she passed out on them they had to take the place apart."

"Interesting guess," Lawson said after a moment.

"You got a better one?" Thompson asked him.

Lawson didn't have to answer that question because at that moment Linda Zazkowski came into the office. She was carrying a small, flat package wrapped in brown paper. Lawson identified himself. He was surprised by what appeared to be a nice girl, deeply distressed by the death of a friend. His notion of a hooker was someone tougher and more callous. She handed in the package.

"It's in a frame," she said. "Nora always kept it on her dressing table."

Lawson unwrapped the package and found himself looking at a studio photograph of a handsome, blond boy with a relaxed, engaging smile. If anyone had seen Eddie Sands at the Beaumont, this excellent picture would surely be a help.

"I came back here from St. Vincent's," she said. "Nora was—was still alive. I wanted to be sure no one messed with her things, because I knew she wouldn't be back for a long time. Oh, my God, Sergeant, who did it?"

"I wish I could tell you," Lawson said. "Maybe you can help."

"How?"

"The sergeant's playing guessing games," Thompson said.

"You were her friend," Lawson said, still deadpan. "You visited her apartment often, according to Mark Haskell, who talked to you at the hospital."

"I heard on the radio he was attacked, too," Linda asked. "How is he?"

"He's fine. Lump on his head. He happened to be lucky."

"What kind of monster—"

"About the apartment, Miss Zazkowski."

"I often went there on Sundays," she said. "That's our day off. We were friends, good friends."

"It wasn't an ordinary burglary," Lawson said. "The kind of things simple thieves take weren't touched. There was a TV set, a hi-fi system in the boy's room. Things like that can be sold on the black market. They weren't taken. Someone was looking for something that could be kept in small places, drawers, hidden away in the upholstery, in the bedding. The killer-thief was looking for one special object. Do you have any idea what it might have been?"

Linda shook her head.

"Did she have a valuable piece of jewelry?"

"Just fake stuff, stage stuff," Linda said.

"She never mentioned anything special, valuable, important that she might have hidden?"

"I don't understand. Like what?"

"Like something she had on somebody," Thompson said. "Something she had on somebody like Stan Nelson."

Linda shook her head, puzzled. "In all the time I knew her she never mentioned Stan Nelson to me until we heard him singing on his telethon on Friday night. I never knew about her and him until then."

Lawson wasn't a stupid man. He'd heard my account of my drink with Linda. He'd heard what she'd told me about the "picture palaces" and the "blackmail factory." He didn't mention it to her then. She might not be safe if Thompson knew she'd been talking.

"I'm grateful for the picture," he said. "It may turn out to be very useful."

I'M NOT A GUY WHO LIKES to be shut away from the action. About two hours of that Sunday afternoon spent trying to remember something that didn't want to surface had me climbing the wall. Doc Partridge must have been right; I had a thick skull. The back of my head felt tender to the touch, but not being able to recall something that apparently wasn't there was giving me a real headache. Everybody else who mattered in the Beaumont was doing something useful. I was just doodling on a legal pad. My best product was a cartoon of what Victoria Haven should have looked like sixty years ago—all bosoms and legs!

I phoned Chambrun in his office.

"I've got to get out of here," I told him.

"You don't like being safe?" he asked.

"Safe and sane don't go together," I told him. "Look, if I circulate a little, boss, talk to people who were around on Friday, it might trigger something. Just sitting here looking at the skyline is for the birds. Let me get back in my own territory."

"I'll talk to Hardy," he said.

Ruysdale had brought me a summer suit, among other things, and I was dressed and ready to go places when Sergeant Lawson appeared up on the roof.

"I hear you're getting restless," he said.

"Not getting—am!" I said.

"The lieutenant thinks you might be useful circulating," Lawson said. "You know everyone. The lieutenant thinks staff people may talk to you more freely than they will to cops or even to Chambrun, the boss.''

"The only one who won't talk to Chambrun is someone who's guilty of something," I said. "People trust him and he's earned that trust."

"I used to think everyone who was innocent would trust us cops," Lawson said. "It turns out they're more certain the criminals will punish them if they talk than they are that we can protect them. We've got a crazy killer circulating here. Better not to talk if you suspect something. They may get what Camargo got and what you almost got."

"And what Nora Sands and the boy got," I said.

Lawson was carrying a briefcase and he unzipped it and took out a framed photograph.

"The Sands kid," he said. "Ms. Zazkowski produced it."

"Who?"

"Your friend Linda Zazkowski."

"So that's her last name." I looked down at the picture of the boy. "Nice-looking lad."

"More important, do you recognize him?" Lawson asked. "You were circulating in the ballroom during the telethon."

Something else to try to remember. I'd had no reason to study the faces of the yammering kids in the ballroom. My job had been to make sure everything was functioning properly, and to be available when an important big shot dropped by to make a contribution. When someone is making a gift of a few thou-

sand dollars he likes to be noticed, I find. I would greet
him and make sure he was maneuvered into range of
the TV cameras, make sure his name was pronounced
right. The kids didn't matter. They were just part of
the scenery. I handed the photograph back to Lawson. "No dice," I said.

"Like to take me across the roof while I show this
to Stan Nelson and his guys?" Lawson asked. "I'd
like to get your reaction to their reaction."

It was something positive to do. We started across
the roof, only to be greeted by Toto with that "They
shall not pass!" snarl on his face. Victoria Haven
stepped out of her place, smiling.

"No one approaches me that I'm not warned," she
said. "Toto!" The little dog eased away, muttering to
himself. I introduced Lawson.

"You weren't at the telethon on Friday, were you,
Mrs. Haven?" he asked.

"The risk of being trampled to death at my age is
not inviting," Mrs. Haven said. "From five to seven
Friday afternoon I was in the Trapeze bar as usual—
with Toto. People who gave big money dropped in
there to be admired. After that I watched the show on
television."

Lawson showed her the framed picture of Eddie
Sands. "Didn't happen to see this boy, did you?"

She took the picture. "Nora Sands' son?" She
studied it for a second or two. "He doesn't look even
remotely like Stan Nelson."

"You thought he might?"

"I hear rumors, like anyone else," Mrs. Haven said. She handed back the pictures. "I'm afraid I can't be any help, Sergeant."

We left her with her Japanese bodyguard and went on to Penthouse number three. Butch Mancuso answered our ring at the doorbell.

"It's about time," he said to Lawson. "We've been locked in here long enough, Sergeant. You finally decided to turn us loose?"

"Not my decision to make," Lawson said. "I'm here to show you three men something."

Stan Nelson and Johnny Floyd were right behind Mancuso. Lawson handed them the picture.

"Nora's boy?" Stan asked. He looked at the picture for what seemed a long time, and then handed it back. "If he asked me for an autograph I don't remember it." He gave us a sort of sad smile. "I've often wondered about him. I suppose I've wondered if there might be a chance that he—well, you know the talk."

"Looks about as much like you as I do," Johnny Floyd said.

"None of you noticed him at the telethon? You have to take a minute to write even the little that you did on the pledge card, Nelson. It must be routine to look at the person who asks you to sign, give them a smile."

"There were hundreds of them," Johnny Floyd said.

Stan nodded. "They become a kind of sea of faces after a while," he said. "I've tried to put this together for myself, Sergeant. From what Nora told us, and what Mark Haskell here found out when he went down to the Village, the boy played stickball Friday until dark. It gets dark about eight-thirty. If he came up here after that to get an autograph it had be nine or nine-thirty at the earliest. I would have been at the telethon for better than twenty-one hours at that time. I was damn near dead on my feet by then. Signing an autograph then could have been automatic, almost like in a trance. I probably wouldn't have recognized my own wife if she'd handed me something to sign.''

"He could have been here much earlier on," Lawson said. "Say, right after the telethon started at midnight on Thursday. His mother would have been at work, wouldn't know that he'd left the apartment to come up here. You'd have been fresh then. You might remember.''

"This is a dead end, Sergeant," Stan said. "I had no reason to pay special attention to anyone except the big giver, people representing corporations and foundations. I could give you a list of those, plus a few politicians and others who wanted to be noticed. But a fifteen-year-old kid would just be a part of a big blur. It shouldn't be that way, I suppose. A boy with a dollar to give is just as important in a moral sense as an executive with a check for five grand from his company. Unfortunately the kid isn't noticed the same way. Yes, I thank them and smile at them, but notice or remember? No way.''

"Our anonymous informant still keeps pointing at you, Mr. Nelson," Lawson said. "Why, do you suppose?''

"Because he's both anonymous and crazy," Stan said.

"And maybe not so anonymous," Johnny Floyd said, in his harsh, rasping voice. "Maybe his name is Zachary Thompson and he's still out to get Stan for what happened long ago."

Lawson took back the framed picture and slipped it into his briefcase. "I've just come back from talking to Thompson," he said.

"And?" Stan asked.

"He's not your best friend, Mr. Nelson," Lawson said.

THREE

I FOUND I WAS LIVING a totally new experience when I left the roof with Sergeant Lawson and went down with him to Chambrun's office. The last time I'd been on that second floor, where my own apartment was located, I'd been clobbered. There was my office at one end of the corridor, then the linen room and a housekeeper's quarters on either side of my apartment, and then Chambrun's suite of offices, which took up half the space on that section of the second floor, and a bank of elevators, four shafts wide. It had been the safest and most relaxed place in the world for me for years. The people who came and went were mostly staff, friends, co-workers. Hotel guests or customers off the street didn't wander around this small section of our world. If they had business with Chambrun they went to his office. If they had business with me they came into mine. There were no shops or bars to attract anyone. Normally, when I hit that second-floor corridor I would let my breath out, relaxing from the high-speed functioning of the rest of our world. I might even loosen my tie and undo the collar button on my shirt. On this floor I didn't have to make "an appearance"—the smart, well-dressed director of public relations in the world's top luxury hotel.

But here was where I'd been creamed, probably saved from death by the unscheduled appearance of Alec Watson, Jerry Dodd's man, who'd kept me from joining Tony Camargo somewhere in a pine box. It wasn't home-sweet-home anymore, even on a quiet Sunday afternoon. A madman with a club or an iron bar could be lurking behind each door we passed. I was grateful for Sergeant Lawson's company.

Chambrun was in his office, along with Lieutenant Hardy and Betsy Ruysdale. The top of the Man's carved, Florentine desk was littered with papers.

Chambrun looked up at me and his smile was wry. "I would have told you to stay put, at least until tomorrow," he said. "Doc Partridge seems to think you could do yourself more harm fretting than being up and around. Walter thinks you could be useful." He nodded at the lieutenant. "Ruysdale makes the most sense of all of us. She thinks you should collect one of your girl friends and take off for Bermuda, or Canada, or the South Sea Islands until we have our man locked up."

"You go with me, Ruysdale?" I asked. She gave me a Mona Lisa smile and went back to sorting papers. "Then it's no deal. How can I help?"

Chambrun and Hardy were more interested in Lawson. He reported no luck with the picture, with me, Mrs. Haven, and Stan Nelson and his crew. "The next thing is to try the technical people who were in the ballroom during the telethon, camera crews for the TV and film people. One of them may have got a picture of the boy."

"They edit those films," I said. "The boy could have wound up, as the struggling actor complains, on the cutting-room floor—swept up in the trash. So what if he was in the background of a picture?"

"It would prove he was here," Chambrun said. "Here, alive and well."

"We're going into Sunday evening," Hardy said, "but we're still back at Friday as far as the boy is concerned. We know how he got into the Health Club, but where was he shot and when? Square one."

"So how can I help?" I said again.

"Step number two, going back to Friday, is to try to determine who took an impression of the Health Club keys," Chambrun said. "It would seem that it must have happened in the last forty-five minutes or so of Camargo's shift. That was when Jimmy Heath was playing squash with Mr. Shuttleworth. If Camargo wanted to leave the office then, to start his closing routines, someone would have gone into the office and made the impressions."

"Why didn't he just take the key?" I asked.

Chambrun looked at me as if I was a not bright kid in the second grade. "Because if the keys were missing when Camargo and Jim Heath were ready to leave they'd have reported it to Jerry Dodd. We'd have had someone watching for trouble." Chambrun moved restlessly in his chair. "Standard practice. There's always someone in the office, except for a minute or two, here and there, during that last forty-five minutes. A member comes in earlier on to go through whatever his routine is. He says hello to whoever's in the office and that someone, Camargo or Jim Heath on that shift, signs him in on the clipboard sheet. When he leaves he goes out the same way, past the office. Ten to one he says 'goodnight' to whoever's in the office. If it was a stranger he would probably remember, be able to give us some sort of description. We've gotten in touch with all but three of the people who used the club during that evening shift on Friday night. Mr. Shuttleworth, the last man to leave, is away somewhere for the weekend. Ditto Mr. Fessler, the other squash player. Mr. Crowder, a member who went through the gym routines, is also out of town. All the others saw Camargo or Jim Heath when they left. It may be tomorrow before we can catch up with those three we haven't reached. One of them may have the answer we need."

"One hopes to God!" Hardy said.

"I'm puzzled by something, Mr. Chambrun," Betsy Ruysdale said. "It may not mean anything, but—"

"If it puzzles you it means something," Chambrun said.

"I have these clipboard sheets," Ruysdale said. "I went back in the files for other Friday nights to see if they had pretty much the same group of customers each Friday night."

"And do they?"

"I guess you'd say that, more than any other time, the Friday night people are regulars. Mr. Shuttleworth, Mr. Fessler, and Mr. Crowder are always there late."

"So what's puzzling?"

Ruysdale put down several sheets in front of the Man. "Look at the top of the sheet, Mr. Chambrun. Camargo signs it there with the time he took over. Look at the daytime sheet, and you see that Carl Hulman signs at the top and the time he opened up in the morning. Now, this last Friday night we have a sheet with the names of the members and guests who came in. It's signed at the top by Tony Camargo, like always. But at the bottom of this sheet are his initials, T.C."

"So, he closed up shop and initialed it," Chambrun said.

"But not the Friday before that, or the Friday before that," Ruysdale said. "No initials to close out. No initials on the bottom of Hulman's sheets. It wasn't common practice for anyone to initial the sheet at the bottom."

Chambrun shuffled through the sheets she handed him. He looked up at her. "You think?"

"Could they be the initials of someone who came into the club—the last person to come in?"

"They're Camargo's initials," Chambrun insisted.

"But if he never initialed the sheets before?"

"If it was a last member to come in, why not his full name?"

"I don't know, Mr. Chambrun," Ruysdale said. "It could be someone who wasn't a member, a guest-customer. Maybe someone who works in the hotel, someone he knew well and just made a record of it, automatically? It may mean nothing at all, but—"

"Get Jim Heath up here," Chambrun said. "And get me our employees' file, everyone whose name begins in C."

"On the double," Ruysdale said, and took off for her own office.

"Ring any bell with you, Mark?" Chambrun asked.

No kind of bells seemed to be ringing for me that afternoon. I tried, off the top of my head, to think of someone on our staff of hundreds of people whose initials were T.C.

"Mike Maggio," I suggested. Mike is our night bell captain, a friend of Tony Camargo's I knew, and a very bright guy who knows everything that goes on in the hotel during his shift.

"Get him," Chambrun said.

I picked up the phone on his desk, called the front office and told them the boss wanted Mike.

"You think this adds up to something, Pierre?" Hardy asked.

"It's your kind of nit-picking, Walter. Wouldn't you follow it up?"

The red light blinked on Chambrun's phone. I answered. It was Ruysdale from the front office. "Officer Scott, one of Hardy's men, is out here with a young woman."

"That'll be the girl Camargo was dating," Sergeant Lawson said.

She was about five feet tall, with bright red hair and a little-girl face. She was clearly out of her skull with fear. Scott was just another cop, cut out of the same mold as Lawson.

"This is Margradel Rousch," he said to Hardy. "She's the girl Camargo had a date with on Friday night."

Cops surprise me now and then. A city of millions and they find a girl named Margradel who works in a bar somewhere. No trouble.

"I'm Lieutenant Hardy of Homicide, Miss Rousch. You know what's happened to Camargo?"

"The—the radio." It was a whisper.

"You saw him Friday night?"

"It-it was more like Saturday morning," she said. "I—I don't get off till one o'clock."

"You expected him? You had a date with him?"

"Yes."

"There's nothing to be frightened of, Margradel," Chambrun said gently. "The lieutenant just wants to know if Tony talked to you about his job, anything unusual that may have happened Friday night."

"No sir. He didn't."

"Think carefully," Hardy said.

"I—I don't think so. Oh, he said he'd been afraid he'd be late. He—he'd run into an old friend he hadn't seen in a long time. But he wasn't late."

"Did he mention the friend's name?"

"No sir."

"The initials T.C. mean anything to you?" Chambrun asked.

She looked bewildered. "Those are Tony's initials."

"Do you know someone else with those initials?"

The girl shook her head slowly, reaching for something she couldn't find. I knew how she felt. I'd been there all day. "I can't think of anyone," she said.

"Did Tony Camargo ever write you any letters, notes, Miss Rousch?" Hardy asked.

Faint color mounted in her pale cheeks. "Two or three times," she said. I got the impression from looking at her that Tony's note had been something more than casual. He'd had "hot pants" for little Miss Rousch, according to Jimmy Heath.

"How did he sign those notes?" Hardy asked.

"You mean, what did he—?"

"I mean, how did he sign his name."

She moistened her lips. "Just 'Tony,'" she said. "Or—or maybe, 'Your Tony.'"

"Not his initials, T.C.?"

"No sir."

I wanted to ask her if she'd been nice to Tony that last night of his life, but it didn't seem to the point. I imagined she might regret it now if she hadn't.

"One more time, Miss Rousch," Hardy said. "Camargo told you he'd been afraid he'd be late because he'd run into an old friend he hadn't seen in a long time. He didn't say anything about that friend, who he was, where he'd run into him?"

"No sir." The color mounted in her cheeks again. "He—he had other things on his mind."

"Not unusual for a young man with a very pretty date," Chambrun said, smiling at her.

So much for Miss Margradel Rousch. Hardy knew how to reach her if he wanted to talk to her again. He gave Officer Scott orders to send her home in a taxi.

In the doorway she encountered Jimmy Heath on his way in. They apparently didn't know each other.

"That was Tony's girl friend," Chambrun told Jimmy.

"Oh, wow!" Jimmy said. "From the way he described her I'd have expected a lot more—more glamor."

"Glamor is in the eye of the beholder," Chambrun said. "Look at these clipboard sheets, Jimmy."

Jimmy looked at them, frowning. "They seem regular," he said.

"The one for Friday night. The initials at the bottom of the list of people who came in."

"Tony's," Jim said.

"He didn't initial any other sheets," Chambrun said. "If you closed out the clipboard sheet any night did you add your initials?"

"No, Mr. Chambrun. Whoever was at the desk when our shift took over signed at the top. That was almost always Tony. Maybe two or three times in the last six years it was me. Once, way back, Tony was sick and didn't come in at all. A couple of other times Carl Hulman had something to talk to Tony about before he left and I took over the check-ins."

"But no initials?"

"That just wasn't part of the system," Jimmy said.

"How do you account for them, then, on Friday night?"

Jimmy shrugged. "Maybe Tony was just doodling," he said.

"And maybe they're the initials of someone who came in at the very last," Chambrun said. "You think of anyone on the hotel staff with those initials?"

"Not off the top of my head," Jimmy said.

Ruysdale came in from her office with a sheet of paper. "List of employees whose last names begin with C," she said to Chambrun. "I don't find any T.C." She looked at me. "There's a man in my office who wants to talk to you, Mark. He says he's the Reverend Leonard Martin."

"That's the New Morality guy I told you I met at Nora's apartment," I told them all. "He found her. We went to St. Vincent's together."

"Bring him in, Ruysdale," Chambrun said. "I think we'd all like to talk to him."

The Reverend Leonard Martin had changed out of his smart tan gabardine suit into something dark, dark tie, black shoes. Probably his Sunday suit, I thought. I introduced him to Chambrun and Hardy and Lawson and Jimmy Heath.

"I heard what happened to you on the radio, Haskell," he said to me. "Thank heaven it wasn't more serious."

"There's a man in the hospital with a broken jaw," Chambrun said.

"Monstrous," Martin said. "I came here because I've had no luck with the police, the district attorney, or Zachary Thompson."

"A strange combination," Chambrun said.

"I've been trying to find out what the funeral arrangements are for Nora Sands and her boy. I would gladly conduct services for them. If not that, I would like to be present to pay my respects."

"I don't think arrangements have been made as yet," Chambrun said. "Stan Nelson has offered to pay expenses, but there isn't anybody, really, to accept."

"After their past it's rather decent of him," Martin said.

Chambrun and Hardy exchanged looks, and the unspoken decision was made that the ball was in Chambrun's court.

"We have three people murdered and an attempt at a fourth, Mr. Martin," Chambrun said. "Anyone who had contact with those people could be helpful to us."

"Any way I can be," Martin said.

"You didn't know Tony Camargo, did you? Anthony Camargo? He worked for me here in the hotel. He was the second victim."

"His name on the radio," Martin said. "That's all."

"Show Mr. Martin the picture," Chambrun said to Lawson.

Lawson took the picture out of his briefcase and handed it to the minister. A spasm of pain contracted Martin's face. "Nora's boy," he said. "What a tragedy! A lovely, well-mannered, nice, open kid."

"You knew him?"

"As I told Haskell, I had supper at Nora's apartment a couple of Sunday evenings. The boy was there both times."

"Forgive me, Mr. Martin, if I seem a little puzzled by your relationship with Nora Sands," Chambrun said. "Your movement, your cause—it's called the New Morality?—was aimed at putting the Private Lives Club, its world of pornography, and Zachary Thompson out of business. Yet you became friendly enough with Nora Sands, a key figure in Zachary's business, to visit with her, take supper with her in her own home. She was the enemy, wasn't she?"

Martin gave Chambrun what looked to me like a patronizing smile. "Our primary responsibility in this life, Mr. Chambrun, is to redeem the evildoer, to save him, if possible, from eternal damnation."

"Even if your evidence is a very attractive and tempting female?" Chambrun said. "In the brief time that I saw her I wasn't blind to Miss Sands' charm."

Martin looked down at those well-manicured fingertips of his. "Imagine the mark she might have made in this world if she'd taken the right road in the beginning. Some people are blessed with a special magnetism and vitality that makes for power. Nora Sands had that power and she used it to tempt men onto the path of evil. Imagine what she might have been able to give to a good man in the way of support and help."

I sensed Chambrun's impatience with that kind of talk.

"I'm afraid we are more interested in discussing facts, Mr. Martin, than we are with the 'might-have-been,'" Chambrun said. "When did you begin your

crusade against Zachary Thompson's world of pornography?"

"It's all around you, all the time," Martin said.
"You can't walk into a family drugstore or your local
newsstand without seeing his magazine on display."

"And others like it," Chambrun said. "Thompson's empire is only one of several. There's a public
demand for what he peddles. If there wasn't he would
have to bootleg it, like liquor in the twenties.
Shouldn't you be taking aim at that public appetite?"

"Man is weak, has always been weak," Martin said.
"But it's not just the pictures of nude women in suggestive poses with which I'm concerned. It's the
women themselves and the purposes for which they're
used."

"Professional sex?" Chambrun said.

"Criminal purposes," Martin said, his voice hard-
ening.

"The word 'criminal' interests me, Mr. Martin,"
Lieutenant Hardy said.

"And should, Lieutenant. And should!"

"One of the girls from the Private Lives Club, a
friend of Nora Sands', who came to St. Vincent's when
you and Haskell were there waiting for a report on
Nora Sands' condition, talked about blackmail, about
what she called 'picture palaces.' Is that what you're
talking about, Mr. Martin?" Chambrun asked.

"Do you know that all across the country there are
men of importance in their communities who are paying huge sums of money into Thompson's pockets for
having been tempted into one fall from grace? And

there is no way to get them to take action against that creature because they would be destroyed by pictures taken of them in a moment of degradation.''

"How did you propose to entrap him, Mr. Martin? Did you plan to let yourself be caught with one of Thompson's girls and then expose him and damn the torpedoes?''

"Good God, no!'' Martin said. "I had no solid plan except to observe and look for a way. I thought if I could locate one of these 'picture palaces' I might save some poor devil from disaster, and at the same time have something on which the police and the district attorney could act.''

"And no luck?''

"Zachary Thompson is no fool,'' Martin said. "I am not a totally unknown figure. The New Morality is a public cause. The first time I walked into that Private Lives Club they knew who I was and why I might be there.''

"So you had lost before you began,'' Chambrun said.

"I knew at once that they would play it safe while I was there,'' Martin said. "So I went there, night after night. I could out-wait them, I thought. They would get careless, I thought.''

"And they aimed one of their best weapons at you, Nora Sands,'' Chambrun said.

"At first she just turned on her charm as a hostess,'' Martin said. "She knew who I was, had seen one or two of my New Morality rallies on television. Right from the start she made it clear she knew why I was there. She never once tried to make me believe they weren't doing in that club what I knew they were doing. There was no cat-and-mouse. All right out in the open."

"And you aren't used to sinners who are open and aboveboard about their sins," Chambrun said. The tone of his voice should have told Martin that respect was not one of the Man's feelings at the moment.

"I am used to people who repent their sins," Martin said. "That's at the core of the whole Christian ethic, repentance."

"And did Nora Sands put on a repentance act for you, to divert you from your primary purpose?"

"On the contrary, she talked about her past and her present with delight, like someone describing a whole series of wonderful surprise parties," Martin said. "She wasn't impressed when I talked to her about the Day of Judgment. 'Now is what I care about, Reverend,' she told me. 'I'll take my chances on the Hereafter when I get there.' I—well, I must admit, I became more concerned for a time with trying to save this one lost woman than I was with destroying Zachary Thompson's filthy business."

"Samson and Delilah," Chambrun said.

"In a way," Martin said, ignoring what he must have sensed was contempt. "My—my priorities were altered. I wanted to change her, to save her. Tearing down the Temple could come later."

"Oh, brother!" Chambrun said. "And then?"

"We talked about everything. Her growing up, my youth. She tried to persuade me to 'take her out on the

town,' away from the Private Lives Club. I knew she
wanted to get me away from there so that they could
carry on their regular business without my observing.
I refused.''

"It must have been one of the few times a healthy
male ever said 'no' to her,'' Chambrun said.

"She understood my commitment,'' Martin said.
"Then she invited me to her apartment one Sunday,
the day the club was closed. 'I'll make you supper
while you wrestle with my soul, Leonard,' she said. I
suspected she might try to tempt me into a violation of
my principles, but when I arrived the boy was there.
He never left.''

"A disappointment, I suspect,'' Chambrun said.

"Only in that I couldn't talk to her about the mat-
ters that were important to me,'' Martin said.

"Her salvation?''

"Of course. What did happen was that I discovered a whole new aspect of that extraordinary woman.
In addition to what I knew she was, she was a mother,
deeply concerned with her son, tender, loving. Would
you believe we spent most of the evening talking about
baseball, his passion? I'd had some of the same interests when I was a kid, and I could talk his language. I
left there without having spoken one word that I had
come there to speak.''

"But you went again?''

"Yes. And the boy was there again, and it was the
same.''

"Disappointed?''

"In a way," Martin said. "But I sensed that the way I got along with the boy pleased her. I have to admit that it pleased me to please her."

"There were more times?"

"Just those two times," Martin said. "The second one was only last Sunday."

"And during the week you continued to go every night to the Private Lives Club, hoping someone's foot would slip?" Chambrun said.

Chambrun nodded. "She never left me when I was there. I began to suspect that while she kept my attention on her they'd found a way to operate as usual. Male customers came and went, drank at the bar, talked with the girls. I never saw one of the girls leave with a man and assignations were arranged for the girls to meet them later in one of Thompson's hide-outs."

Lieutenant Hardy broke in. "In all of this time, Mr. Martin, did Miss Sands ever mention anyone, a man, she'd had trouble with? Did she suggest she'd ever been involved in one of these blackmail schemes you've mentioned and that someone was out to punish her for it?"

"No, and I don't think she ever was," Martin said. "Not, at least, in recent years. She talked about working for Thompson out on the West Coast when she was eighteen. Perhaps then. Then she met and fell in love with Stan Nelson, the singer. He taught her, she told me, how much fun it was to have sex for pleasure rather than being paid for it. She was frighteningly frank about herself, Lieutenant. 'You could offer me a thousand dollars to make love to you, Leonard,' she told me once, 'and I'd say no. But if I thought it would be fun with you it would be yours for the asking."

"And did you ask?" Chambrun inquired.

"You must know that I didn't, that I couldn't," Martin said. "It would have been against all my precepts, my rules for living."

"It seems you missed a golden opportunity," Chambrun said, the edge on his voice cutting.

"I don't particularly like your attitude toward me, Mr. Chambrun," Martin said.

"This woman you played games with is violently dead," Chambrun said. "You were a self-appointed investigator and you spent hours and days at it. You haven't come up with one single fact from the investigation that is any use to us. Let me ask you a far-out question. Do you know anyone whose initials are T.C.? Someone who worked at the Private Lives Club? Someone Nora Sands mentioned in her marathon conversations with you about her past and present?"

"T.C.," Martin said. "I don't think so. Wait! There was a baseball player who was one of the kid's heroes of the past, Tony Conigliaro."

"Who would have shot the boy, clubbed Tony Camargo and Nora to death, and made a try at Haskell?"

"Not very likely," Martin said. "But no other T.C. comes to mind."

Chambrun had had it. He looked at Hardy and gave a little helpless shrug of his shoulders.

"About yesterday, Mr. Martin. I understand from Haskell that you'd heard about the murder of Eddie Sands on the radio. You tried to reach Nora Sands on the telephone but you kept getting a busy signal on her phone."

Martin nodded. "I knew she needed a friend, must need help. I went to where she lived on Jane Street. She didn't answer her doorbell, but I thought she might have shut herself away, not wanting to see anyone. The janitor fellow let me go upstairs to knock on her door. It was open, and I went in and found her. She was alive but unconscious. I've had some experience with first aid. Her pulse was very weak. I tried mouth to mouth, and then I called 911 for help."

"You had thoughts about what had happened?"

"The apartment was a shambles," Martin said. "Robbery was my first thought."

"And your second?"

"That it must have some connection with what had happened to the boy," Martin said. "There had been talk on the radio about anonymous phone calls pointing to Stan Nelson."

"Did she ever suggest to you that she had something on Nelson?"

"Never. She actually spoke of Nelson with a kind of affection. She tried to sue him for some of his property when they split up years ago, but I think that was Thompson's advice. I got the notion that she regretted that suit. She was at fault, not Nelson, for what had broken up their thing together."

"I guess that's it, Mr. Martin," Hardy said.

"About the funeral arrangements?" Martin said.

"When there is some decision about them we'll let you know," Hardy said.

Martin hesitated a moment. He didn't seem satisfied. But he nodded to us, turned, and walked slowly out of the office. In the doorway he almost collided with Mike Maggio, our night bell captain. Mike stood aside to let the reverend gentleman out and then he joined us.

"I just came on duty, Mr. Chambrun, and found a message that you wanted me," Mike said.

Mike is a dark, curly-haired Italian with bright black eyes. I think of him as one of the sharpest people on our staff, street smart, never missing anything that goes on in the hotel. I know Chambrun has a special regard for him.

"Maybe you can help us with something, Mike," Chambrun said. He picked up the clipboard sheets from his desk and handed them to Mike. He explained our curiosity about the initials T.C. at the bottom of the Friday night sheet. "We thought at first they were Tony Camargo's, but he never initialed any other sheet like that. Make any sense to you?"

Mike frowned down at the sheet for a moment. "It doesn't seem possible," he said, "but do you remember a guy named Tom Colson who used to work here, Mr. Chambrun?"

"Regrettably, I do," Chambrun said.

I remember Colson, too. It went back three years or more. Colson had been on the maintenance crew, clean-up work in the early hours of the morning. He'd been a brash, smart-aleck kind of a guy. One night someone heard a woman screaming in one of the upper corridors. One of the hotel guests called Security. The Security man arrived upstairs to find Colson unmercifully beating a girl. Colson ran, and they never caught up with him. Chambrun regretted remembering it because it involved two things that were black eyes for his beloved hotel. Violence by an employee was bad enough, but the badly beaten girl was a prostitute who had been satisfying the demands of some hotel guests. Call girls are a fact of life in a modern hotel, whether you care to admit it or not. The police hadn't caught up with Tom Colson, the girl wouldn't say who her customer had been and wouldn't or couldn't explain why Colson had attacked her. The whole thing was swept quietly under the rug, but it was a black mark that none of us involved at the time cared to recall.

"Colson was never called by his last name, or his first name, Tom," Mike Maggio said. "He used his initials. Everyone called him 'T.C.'"

I felt small hairs rising on the back of my neck. I'd never had anything to do with Colson when he worked in the hotel. The clean-up crews in the early hours were not part of my pattern. I don't think I'd exchanged a half-dozen words with him in the four or five years that he'd worked for us. I'd completely forgotten about him until this morning.

"I—I saw Colson yesterday," I said. My mouth felt dry. "He was at St. Vincent's when I went there with

Martin to check out on Nora Sands. He was in the sitting room outside the emergency ward.''

The man in the baseball cap!

FOUR

YOU CAN HAND CHAMBRUN a surprise or a jolt, but he never explodes. I thought there was something a little glacial about his deep-set eyes, but his voice was perfectly calm—almost too calm.

"You say you saw this Colson fellow—T.C.—yesterday at St. Vincent's, and yet you've never mentioned it?"

I nodded. "Because I didn't put the face and the name together," I said. "I suppose it's been four years since I last saw him."

"Three years and seven months," Chambrun said. He remembered the exact date of Colson's violence with the call girl.

"I never had any dealings with Colson when he worked here," I said. "You could say he wasn't in my orbit. 'Hello,' or 'Goodnight' or something like that, no more. I didn't know, till Mike just told us, that he was called T.C. If it was mentioned back there—three years and seven months ago—I didn't recall it."

"Never mind the apologies, Mark. About seeing him—?" Chambrun asked.

I repeated my story of going to talk to Eddie Sands' stickball friend, and from there to Jane Street where I found cops and an ambulance and the Reverend Leonard Martin with his horror story about Nora

Sands. Martin and I had gone on to the hospital and waited outside the emergency ward for some news.

"I noticed this guy sitting across from me, smiling at me as if I should know him. There was something familiar about him, but I couldn't place him. He was wearing a baseball cap, with the peak pulled down over his forehead. Of course I'd never seen T.C. with any kind of a cap on. I had no reason to be thinking about something that happened here in the hotel years ago. I—I was pretty shaken up by what had happened to Nora. I went out to telephone you about what had happened. When I came back I looked for the guy in the baseball cap, thinking I might be able to place him, but he was gone. I didn't think about him again. There was too much else cooking."

"He saw that you hadn't placed him," Chambrun said, "came back here and waited for you to show up so he could polish you off before you did remember." He picked up the phone on his desk. "Get Jerry Dodd up here," he told the switchboard operator.

"What do you suppose he was doing at the hospital?" Hardy asked.

"He had just beaten up Nora Sands and ransacked her apartment," Chambrun said. "He had to know whether she was dead, or whether she'd been able to tell the doctors or the cops who had attacked her. He didn't expect to see anyone there he knew, and suddenly, there was Mark, who sooner or later would remember him. When Mark walked past him to go to the phone he realized that for the moment he was safe. He came back here to make sure he stayed safe."

"But this clip sheet with his initials on it goes back to the day before that, Mr. Chambrun," Mike Maggio said.

"You don't have to be a handwriting expert to know that those initials were written by Tony Camargo," Chambrun said. "Look at the other names—same capital T., same capital C. Colson, or T.C., walked into the Health Club and encountered an old friend, Tony Camargo. Tony did an automatic, he put down the name of a customer on the clipboard sheet. Maybe he didn't know his name, just what he'd always been called—T.C."

"Put it down and never mentioned it to anyone, a guy he knew was wanted for an old crime?" Mike said. "That doesn't fit with what I know of Tony Camargo."

"Who knows what kind of line T.C. fed Tony," Chambrun said. "He'd come back to clear himself? He needed time? He needed some sort of favor from Tony."

"But he came to get the keys," Hardy said.

Chambrun nodded. "He knew the routines. He knew if he waited around he'd probably be left in the office alone for a few minutes. Tony was willing to help, but he was also in a hurry to get the place closed up. He had a date with a pretty little redhead, Miss Margradel Rousch. He left T.C. alone in the office and when he came back T.C. was gone."

"With a wax impression of the keys," Hardy said.

"He must have told Tony where he could be reached," Chambrun said. "Tony didn't bother then, because he had a date. After his date he went home and slept late. We woke him up with a phone call about finding a dead man in the pool."

"And he didn't mention T.C. then," Mike said.

"Didn't connect the two things. He did tell Scotty McPherson that he was on his way 'to see a guy.' I suspect that 'guy' was T.C. Tony was giving him a chance to prove whatever it was he'd sold Tony on, before he reported that T.C. had been around the hotel again. T.C. made sure Tony never got the chance to make that report."

"If you're right, this T.C. is a crazy psychotic," Hardy said.

"He's that, whether I'm right or wrong," Chambrun said. "We know that from three years and seven months ago. Interesting pattern. He beats up a prostitute back then, would probably have killed her if he hadn't been interrupted. He kills the son of a prostitute last Friday. He kills Nora on Saturday, a woman of the same profession. He kills Tony to cover that crime, and tries to kill Mark for the same reason. That's all madness out of this world!" He brought his fist down on his desk top. "So while we're playing games I'll make you a bet, Walter. The best steak dinner, with drinks and wine, that the Beaumont can provide says that we have another name for T.C."

"Another name?"

"Mr. Anonymous!" Chambrun said. "I should have to give you odds it's so certain."

Jerry Dodd arrived at that point and listened to Chambrun's theory. He clearly accepted it as gospel.

"The sonofabitch is on a killing binge," he said. "I wonder what sets him off?"

"Money," Mike Maggio said. "I knew this guy well enough during some four years he worked here to hate his guts!" He glanced at Chambrun. "You hired him, Mr. Chambrun, so I kept my mouth shut."

"I should have that printed on a sign and hung on the wall over there," Chambrun said. "Every time I get to thinking I'm pretty hot stuff I should look at it. 'You hired T.C.'" His eyes widened. "Do you know who recommended him? Tony Camargo! Which explains why Tony was prepared to help him in some way on Friday night. Old friend."

"Soft-touch Tony," Jerry Dodd said.

"He wouldn't have knowingly betrayed Mr. Chambrun," Mike Maggio said. "But he would have tried to help someone he thought was a friend."

"You said 'money,' Mike," Chambrun said.

"I'd bet my shirt he's working for someone," Mike said. "You mentioned a 'hit man.' That's what T.C. is, a crazy hit man. There's no profit for him in this killing spree. He wouldn't run the risk of circulating in the Beaumont unless someone paid him well for it."

"He is the weapon but someone else controls it?" Chambrun suggested.

"The way I see it," Mike said.

"That would seem to eliminate Stan Nelson," Hardy said, "because the anonymous phone calls keep trying to point to him."

"A very shrewd way to make us react just as you have, Walter," Chambrun said. "Right now we have another problem, however. He can be circulating still, God knows where, in the hotel. I want every inch of the place checked out, Jerry, every nail hole!''

"Right,'' Jerry said. "There must be twenty-five or thirty people still working here who would know T.C. on sight. We know he was here on Friday night. You were on duty then, Mike.''

"I know,'' Mike said. "You remember what it was like here on Friday night? A thousand screaming creeps everywhere. I had my eyes open for pickpockets and street crumbs. I wasn't looking for T.C. Like Mark, I haven't thought about him for damn near four years!''

"A man wearing a baseball cap in the Beaumont lobby?'' Hardy asked.

"You wouldn't believe the get-up people wear to that telethon,'' Mike said. "All kinds of clothes and almost no clothes.''

Jerry Dodd was poised to take off. "You don't have any reason to suspect T.C. could still be roaming around the hotel, do you, Boss? It's almost twenty-four hours since he tried to get Mark. He could be in Mexico by now.''

Chambrun's heavy eyelids lifted. "There are too many unanswered questions for us to ignore the possibility that he's still in our neighborhood,'' he said. "Why was Eddie Sands killed here, or brought here after he was killed? To implicate Stan Nelson—because that seems to be part of the plan? Because it is a safe place for T.C. to operate because he knows every inch of the place? Because, as Mike suggests, he is be-

ing paid by someone whose base is here in the hotel—
like Stan Nelson? A man who knows the geography of
this building could stay hidden here indefinitely, Jerry,
moving from place to place as you search for him.
And he is just crazy enough to enjoy watching us get
nowhere. I suggest that when you've searched some
unlikely place and not found him that you check back
on that place again. He will think he's safe in some
place you've already searched.''

"On my way," Jerry said, and took off.

Chambrun looked at me. "I still think you should
stay up in my penthouse, Mark," he said.

"Why? I've remembered," I said.

"To this madman you may still be unfinished business," Chambrun said. "We can't expect there'll be
any rhyme or reason to what he does next."

SUNDAY EVENING is normally quiet in the Beaumont.
The Blue Lagoon nightclub is dark on Sundays, the
main dining room serves a buffet supper, a reduced
staff handling it, the Trapeze bar on the mezzanine is
primarily a hangout for business people in the area
and the regulars are not in their offices on Sundays.
On that special Sunday night the hotel guests saw
nothing out of the ordinary. Perhaps there was a little
more talk in the bars and the restaurants about the violence of the last forty-eight hours, more curious
questions directed at the staff, but the Stan Nelson
fans had evaporated. The hotel appeared to be at
peace. To an experienced eye like mine there were a
couple of out-of-the-ordinary things about the cli-

mate. There were perhaps a dozen reporters from the newspapers, radio, and television spending the evening in the bars, hoping for something to happen. I saw other faces that shouldn't have been there on a Sunday night. Jerry Dodd had called in his entire security force, day and night shifts, to conduct Chambrun's "nail hole" search for a psychotic killer.

Chambrun had "advised" me to stay up in his penthouse. I knew it wasn't really advice, but an order. There weren't enough cops or security people available to supply me with a bodyguard who would follow me on my usual routines. The roof was impenetrable, with a trusted operator and a cop riding the elevator, and another cop and a security man guarding the fire stairs. On this summer night I could sit out on the terrace and "wish upon a star" if I chose, and not worry about being "unfinished business."

Daylight was finally fading when I did settle down on the terrace with a Jack Daniels on the rocks. Almost instantly I was aware that I had company. First there was a strangled little growl from Victoria Haven's Japanese friend, and then the lady herself, tall and straight, came across the roof from her own penthouse.

"How dare you not come at once to tell me what's going on, Haskell?" she said. She sat down in Chambrun's white wicker chair.

"Drink?" I asked her.

"I've already had my day's allotment," she said. "Tensions and curiosity got me started early. Still—"

"Gin and tonic?" I asked, knowing the answer. I went inside and made her a drink and brought it out to her.

She was looking out at the city, where millions of lights were popping on in a million apartments. "Do you suppose Thomas Edison ever imagined that?" she asked. She took a sip of her drink. "Exactly right. Thanks, Haskell."

"Edison probably thought—"

"Now cut that out, Haskell!" the lady said. "Tell me what's happening."

So I told her how we'd come to put a name to the man we were certain was the killer. I gave her Mike Maggio's theory that he was being paid by someone to perform his violences. I quoted Chambrun on the uselessness to expect any rhyme or reason for whatever his next move might be.

"Pierre is not thinking like himself," Mrs. Haven said.

"Oh?"

"There's always rhyme and reason behind any pattern of behavior, particularly violent patterns," she said. "Once you've determined what triggers a man, then it's child's play to guess what his moves will be. Our Mike Maggio is probably right. Greed is what makes T.C. tick. What's missing is the identity of the person who's paying him for what he's doing. That's where the madness is, Haskell—in the mind of the man who's paying for services. When you know who that is and why he's paying a killer to kill, the rhyme and reason will fall into place."

Toto gave us a throaty warning. Someone was coming our way from the elevator alcove. For just an instant I felt my muscles tense, and then in the shadows I recognized Sergeant Lawson. He had someone with him. As they came into the circle of light thrown by the terrace lamps, I saw that it was Linda, the girl from the Private Lives Club, Nora Sands' friend.

"Chambrun wants you to try to help Miss Zazkowski," Lawson said to me.

I said hello to the girl and introduced her to Mrs. Haven.

"How fascinating," Mrs. Haven said. "You were the Sands girl's friend! You work in the incredible club where she worked! I would very much like to gossip with you about it sometime."

Linda looked at the old woman as though she wasn't quite right. There was, I thought, a change in Linda. Back at St. Vincent's and in the bar where she'd shared drinks with me, I'd thought of her as tough, self-possessed, going her own way and to hell with what I thought of her. Now I thought she looked vulnerable, which made her look younger, frightened, a little helpless.

"Mr. Chambrun says you're very clever at sketching likenesses of people, Haskell," Sergeant Lawson said. "He wondered if you could draw a likeness of this Colson fellow—T.C.—and show it to Miss Zazkowski. She might be able to tell us if he ever circulated at the Private Lives Club."

"I don't do likenesses," I said, "just caricatures."

I picked up the legal pad on which I'd been doodling earlier, tore off the used sheet and put it aside, and tried to recall what I could of T.C. when he worked for us. To be successful with that sort of thing you have to have a feeling about the subject. I remembered an arrogant smile, a kind of swaggering insolence, a sort of "screw you" defiance. I began to play with it, and something happened. I handed the pad to Linda.

"That's libelous!" Mrs. Haven said. She laughed.

I glanced at her and saw she'd picked up the sheet I'd torn off the pad. I'd forgotten that on it was the thing I'd done of her, all bosoms and legs, followed by a smirking little dog. Well, good or bad, she'd recognized herself.

"Done with affection, luv," I said.

"I should hope so!" the lady said.

I turned back to Linda who was frowning at the thing I'd done to T.C. "I'd guess he's about six feet tall, about a hundred and eighty pounds," I said. "Stocky. When I saw him at St. Vincent's his dark hair was longer than it shows in that sketch, but I can't really visualize it long. He had on a baseball cap, so I can't guess how the whole hairdo looks today."

"There's something about this—" Linda said.

"A little like the top guy of a street gang," I said. "I suppose he could be twenty-eight, thirty years old today."

"This brings something back to mind," Linda said. "You say it isn't a likeness, but right away I thought of an incident a couple of weeks ago."

"Tell us," Lawson said.

"The man you were with at St. Vincent's," Linda said to me. "The Reverend Martin?"

"What about him?"

"He's been camping out at the Club for about a month, every night we were open," Linda said. "It was Nora's job to keep him occupied, and she did. We all knew why he was there."

"To get something on you."

"Yes. We've been playing everything pretty close to the vest since he started in. One night he was sitting at a table with Nora—she never left him for a moment—when a man barged in from the street, or maybe from the back somewhere. He wasn't our type of customer."

"What is your type of customer?" Mrs. Haven asked.

"Well dressed, money," Linda said. She gave Mrs. Haven that challenging look I remembered from our drink together. "We're not inexpensive luxuries."

"Oh my!" Mrs. Haven said, sounding delighted.

"The man who barged in," Lawson prompted. "Was it Tom Colson—T.C.?"

"Could have been," Linda said. "This drawing made me think of what happened."

"So what happened?"

"This man—" and Linda tapped my sketch "—was suddenly at the bar. He ordered a drink, something straight in a small glass, then he turned around and looked over the room and the people. He spotted Nora and the Reverend Martin at their table. I—I remember his smile. It was like this." She tapped the sketch again. "He tossed off his drink, put the empty glass down on the bar, and started across the room to Nora's table. She could sense trouble a mile away and I saw her give a little signal to one of the waiters. The man got to the table, reached out, and chucked the astonished Reverend Martin under the chin. 'I hope you'll say one of your sanctimonious prayers for me, you phony old bastard,' he said. The waiter reached him and took him by the arm. The man shook himself free. 'I'm going, I don't need help,' he said. 'This place is a little too rich for my blood.' He sneered down at Martin. 'Sweet dreams, Reverend. If you don't make the lady I'm sure she'll give you a picture to take home to bed with you.' The waiter took him to the front door and gave him a shove out onto the street."

"That's what Haskell's sketch made you think of?" Lawson asked, after a moment.

She nodded.

"Then that is our man?"

"I can't be sure," Linda said. "But this drawing reminds me of a man I *would* know if I saw him again."

"You think he may have been someone working for Zach Thompson?" I asked her.

"Could be, could not be," she said. "You understand, man, I just work here in the New York club. I've never worked anywhere else for Zach. There are all the other clubs and the magazine. I wouldn't know any of the people who work in those places."

"Is it likely that someone working for this Thompson man would deliberately insult a customer?" Mrs. Haven asked.

Linda gave her a look that suggested maybe Mrs. Haven wasn't a senile idiot after all.

"Nora knew a lot of Zach's people from other places," Linda said. "The night this thing happened with the Reverend Martin she saw trouble coming, and, like I told you, signaled one of the waiters. If she knew the man was one of Zach's people I don't think—"

"Your own people can go sour on you if they drink too much or take drugs," Sergeant Lawson said. "Tell me something, Miss Zazkowski. You girls who work for Thompson must constantly be at risk. You take a strange man off to one of Thompson's hideaways, knowing nothing about him. Your customer could be some kind of violent pervert for all you know. What happens if somebody goes off his rocker while you're—while you're entertaining him?" Lawson seemed to have searched for the word "entertaining."

Again that challenging little jut out of her chin. "I know how to take care of myself," Linda said.

"A one-hundred-and-five-pound girl against a big man?"

"We know ways," the girl said.

"I wondered if Thompson might have some strong-arm boys cruising around, ready to help if they were needed. You're too valuable property for Thompson to want you put out of business for a while."

"I've never had any trouble of that kind," Linda said. She held up her right hand with the fingers crossed. "But—"

"But what, Miss Zazkowski?"

That frightened look I'd noticed when she first arrived seemed to take charge of Linda's face again. "I'm already in big trouble," she said. "I talked to Mr. Haskell in that bar across from St. Vincent's and I told him too much," she said. "I was sick with worry for Nora and it all just came out."

"About the 'picture palaces'?" Lawson said.

"Yes. Zach knew I'd had a drink with Mr. Haskell. He probably wondered how much I'd blabbed. Then you grab me out of my apartment and bring me here. Zach knows that by now and he'll put two and two together. You wouldn't be bothering with me unless you thought I could tell you something important. And I could, like names of customers, and—and—"

"And what?" Lawson persisted.

"I could be floating down the Hudson River by breakfast time," Linda said. "Zach won't put up with anyone who talks too much."

"If you've already talked too much hadn't you better tell us the whole thing? If we know it all, there wouldn't be any point in punishing you. It would just add to the charges against him."

"And will you protect the girl, Sergeant?" Mrs. Haven asked.

"Of course," Lawson said, just a trifle too fast, I thought.

The girl's laugh was bitter. "Will you assign a cop to live with me?" She shook her head. "There are so many ways Zach could get back at me if he chose to. And he'd wait his time if he has to."

"You said you could give us the names of customers, but I imagine you won't. You suggested there was something else—?"

She was silent for a moment. "You asked if there was some way we could get help if we had big trouble with a customer," she said finally. "I told Mr. Haskell about the picture palaces. There are three of those. But there are six other apartments, or rooms, in addition to those. All of them—including the picture palaces—are wired. Every word that's spoken in those places is monitored by someone at the club. All a girl would have to do if she was in trouble was to make it clear by what she said and there'd be help in a hurry."

"How do you know this?"

"When I first started to work for Zach a couple of years ago I took my first customer to one of the outside places. When I reported in I got a lecture from Zach about how I'd talked to the john I was entertaining. I'd told the man what Zach thought was too much about where I grew up and stuff. The guy could finger me if he knew too much and wasn't satisfied. You'd be astonished about the men who go out with girls like me. They always want to know how we got started in the business, where we came from—stuff like that. Zach invented a line for me that was complete fiction. I wouldn't want to repeat it to you, because it was designed to excite the customer. I knew then that everything I said and everything the customer said was being heard. The customer might tell me enough for Zach to decide that the next time he should be taken to one of the picture palaces."

"You can give us the addresses of these places?" Lawson asked.

"That would qualify me for a tombstone," Linda said.

"Not if we could put Thompson away," Lawson said.

"You're a dreamer, Sergeant. Zach's operation is so slick. You could go to the club and it will cost you a hundred bucks for a couple of drinks and a steak sandwich. You want to look at pictures of center-fold girls in the raw, that'll cost you another hundred bucks. But that doesn't entitle you to touch, just to look."

"My goodness!" Mrs. Haven said.

"This is not your day, lady," Linda said. "But even in Calvin Coolidge's time you could go to a burlesque show, right on Broadway, and get a free peep for fifty cents. Today you don't have to pay anything. You just stay home and look at a soap opera on TV if you want to see naked people in bed! But if you do your shopping at the Private Lives Club and you want real action, then you have to pay real money for it. But the action doesn't take place there. You pick a girl after looking at her, or her pictures, then she asks you to take her someplace for a drink. You go out with her. If Zach is there he's whistling 'Dixie' at the bar, innocent as a lamb. You made your money deal with

Nora! If you tried to take a shot at Zach he'd tell you he hired these girls as entertainers, had no notion they were involved in prostitution on the side! You could spend a year and you'd never get anything the district attorney could use for a conviction."

"So you couldn't really harm him?" Mrs. Haven said.

"But if he thought I'd tried I'd be lucky to get off with no more than a couple of broken legs," Linda said. "Maybe you can understand, I don't want to turn myself into a target—even if I thought it might square things for Nora. It's too late to matter to her."

Sergeant Lawson evidently decided that was that. "I want to show this to Stan Nelson and his boys," he said, indicating my drawing. "You can come with us, Miss Zazkowski, or if Haskell wants to buy you a drink you can wait for me here."

"Do I have to wait for you to head for home?" Linda asked. "I'm going to have to face the music with Zach, sooner or later. The longer I put it off, the worse the results may be."

"You're free to go," Lawson said. "If you think you need protection I think Lieutenant Hardy would have someone escort you home."

"It's after I get there that the trouble may come," Linda said.

"Your choice," Lawson said.

"A drink might make you feel better," I said to Linda.

"The last drink I had with you got me talking too much," the girl said. "But one good slug of something would help—if you feel like it."

"I'll be back as soon as Nelson and his boys have had a look at this," Lawson said.

"If I'm gone you'll know where to look for me if I don't show up again," Linda said. "In the river!"

Lawson turned and started across the roof toward Penthouse number 3.

"Vodka and tonic, if I remember," I said.

"This is medicinal," the girl said. "If you have a slug of straight bourbon—?"

As I headed for the kitchenette I heard Victoria Haven say to the girl, "I was always an amateur, you know, my dear."

As I poured drinks for the girl, Mrs. Haven, and myself, I realized my own tensions had relaxed. We might not have a case yet against Tom Colson, T.C. to his friends, but there wasn't any doubt he was the man we wanted. There were several dozen people in the hotel who knew T.C. by sight and were looking for him. The place was swarming with cops and extra security. T.C. had run out of room. Up here, under the stars, we couldn't be safer. I had a slight guilty conscience that I wasn't helping in the search, but I was doing what Chambrun wanted me to do.

I took the drinks out on the terrace. I'd poured about three ounces of bourbon into an old-fashioned glass for Linda, and she drank almost half of it in the first swallow. Mrs. Haven was chattering away about when Fifty-second Street was the jazz center of the world, about the fun she'd had at Leon & Eddie's, about how every second brownstone in the block was a speakeasy, about the gangsters and their molls who looked just the way they were portrayed in Warner Brothers movies, about the first time she'd heard the magnificent Lena Horne, and on and on. I knew she was trying to distract Linda from her personal panics.

The girl put down the balance of her drink on the terrace table.

"I'm sorry," she said. "I'm grateful to both of you, but I've got to face the music with Zach. I'll feel better when it's over with."

"I have always found," Mrs. Haven said, "that putting off bad news is better than being brave about it."

"So we are different!" Linda said.

"Just walk straight through the living room to the front door and you'll find yourself in the elevator alcove," I said. "Good luck."

"I may need it," she said.

She walked through Chambrun's penthouse and to the front door. I don't know to this day why I didn't walk to the elevator with her. She wasn't exactly a guest, the police had brought her. She was going out to the policeman who was riding the elevator. There was Mrs. Haven who was a guest. Perhaps I was just plain lazy. Whatever, I sat sipping my drink while Mrs. Haven commented on Linda.

"Somehow you don't expect these professional prostitutes to be like other women," she said. "They sell their bodies for cash on the barrel head. But how is that so different from the rest of us? Down through the ages women have married for social position, wealth, prestige, and power. There's really not much difference between making yourself available for that sort of thing and charging a set fee for it, is there?''

"It could even be more honest," I said. "You don't have to pretend anything that isn't so."

"I think I can look back and say, with some pride, that I never had to pretend anything," Mrs. Haven said. She chuckled. "In the days when I was that impudent drawing you made of me, Haskell, the choices were infinite. I didn't have to pretend."

At that moment the calm of the evening was shattered by the most blood-chilling scream I can ever remember hearing. It rose to a piercing climax and then seemed to be cut off, as though someone had cut a power line.

PERHAPS IT WAS the acoustics, because I thought the scream came from out on the roof. I ran out into the open, looking for the source. At the same moment outside lights were turned on. Mrs. Haven had found the switch inside Chambrun's place, and the lights surrounding Penthouse number 3 came on and I saw Sergeant Lawson, followed by Stan Nelson and his two guys, come running out into the open. It was suddenly daylight-bright, floods aimed to cover the whole area of the roof. Rounding the corner of Chambrun's place I saw her first. Linda was lying flat on her face just outside the elevator alcove. I shouted to Lawson and gestured.

I reached her first. Her face was turned to one side and I could see blood trickling out of the corner of her mouth. I knelt down beside her.

"Linda! For God sake!" I said.

I slid an arm under her, trying to lift her. I saw her eyelids flutter.

"Linda!"

She opened her eyes and looked at me. "Your man," she whispered. "The man you drew!" And then she was heavy against my arm, slipped out.

Lawson and Stan Nelson and the others were there by then. Between us he carried her into Chambrun's place and put her down on the couch. Mrs. Haven was already on the phone calling for Doc Partridge.

"She speak to you?" Lawson asked me.

"Said it was T.C."

"Well, he can't get away," Lawson said, taking his gun out of its holster.

"He couldn't get up here," Mrs. Haven said. She had come over to us from the phone. "Dr. Partridge is on his way. How bad is she?"

"Get Hardy," Lawson said. "Tell him to check the men on the fire stairs and on the elevator. The only way he could get up here is by knocking off one of those teams." He went out again onto the flood-lighted roof, gun at the ready.

I called Chambrun's office and could hear him muttering a string of unprintable words as I told him what had happened.

There was nothing wrong with the operator and the cop on the elevator. They produced Doc Partridge two or three minutes later, and then went down again to collect Chambrun, Hardy, and whoever. No one unaccounted for had come their way, they assured us.

Mercifully, Linda appeared not to be too badly hurt. She had been slugged on the jaw and had a broken tooth to remind her of it for some time. Doc Partridge administered some kind of smelling salts and she was just beginning to show signs of life when Chambrun, Hardy, and a couple of Hardy's men joined us in the already crowded living room.

Talking a little thickly through swollen lips Linda told us what had happened. She'd walked through this room to the front door, stepped out into the elevator alcove, and there he was.

"The man you drew on your pad, Haskell," she managed to say. "The man I told you about who insulted the Reverend Martin at Zach's club."

Chambrun and Hardy had to be brought up to date on that story.

"No question, Linda?" Chambrun asked.

"I—I'd know him anywhere," she said. "I guess I started to scream and he took a step toward me—and he hit me because I blacked out."

"Brass knuckles," Chambrun said.

"You didn't see him go," Hardy said.

She shook her head. It hurt her to talk. Mrs. Haven had provided her with a Kleenex to hold to her bleeding mouth.

Lawson had rejoined us. "Guys on the fire stairs are okay," he said. "Seen no one, coming or going. They couldn't hear the girl scream because the door to the roof was closed. Peaceful as a wake out there on the stairs."

"I want those men and the two on the elevator replaced," Hardy said. "I want to talk to the four who are on duty now. Someone has sold us out. No other way this T.C. could get up here."

"That's a waste of time, Walter," Chambrun said. "I can vouch for my elevator operator and my security man. Your two men could only sell us out over their dead bodies."

"It's touching of you to be so certain of your own people," Hardy said. He was angry. "There's no other way this character could have got up here."

"There was no way he could get Eddie Sands' body into the Health Club swimming pool, but he did," Chambrun said. "There's no way he could get up here, but he did."

"Up the outside of the building?" Hardy asked.

"If he's a human fly," Chambrun said.

"So he's still got to be up here somewhere," Hardy said. "Has your place been searched, Mrs. Haven?"

"I hope not!" the old lady said. "It's a mess."

"He could be there," Hardy said. "He could have slipped into the back rooms here, or the back room in number three."

Half an hour later we knew for certain that T.C. was no longer on the roof—if he ever had been. Hardy came up with the theory that Linda had been "jumpy." She'd been thinking and talking about T.C. and when she got a quick glimpse of someone in the shadows she imagined it as T.C.

"But it was someone, Walter," Chambrun said. "She didn't knock herself out. How did 'someone' get up here?"

"It was that man!" Linda insisted. "I didn't dream it, I saw him!"

Hardy was looking at Nelson, Mancuso, and Johnny Floyd.

Chambrun laughed. "You can't force the wrong key into a lock, Walter," he said. "Your man Lawson was with Nelson, Mancuso, and Floyd when the girl screamed."

Hardy was steaming. "For once your happy faith in your people has to be misplaced, Pierre," he said. "You made a mistake with this T.C. character years ago. You've made another one now. It's the only answer."

"And you don't trust your people?" Chambrun asked.

"How can I, when one of them must have had a price," the lieutenant said.

"There's nothing more I can do for this young woman," Doc Partridge said. "Her next stop is the dentist."

Chambrun had gone to the phone. I couldn't hear what he was saying but I imagined he was warning Jerry Dodd that T.C. had been up here and was now gone. He still had to get out of the hotel. Jerry would have every possible exit guarded. I knew.

Somehow that wasn't comforting. T.C., our crazy killer, had us all on edge. He wasn't anywhere on the roof, but he had a way of turning up where he couldn't be. I found myself staying out of line of the window, half expecting to see that grinning face looking in at us from the outside. It wasn't possible because the roof was swarming now with Hardy's people and yet T.C. had us all buffaloed. The crazy bastard didn't need a reason for another violence. He was on some kind of psychotic binge. I had a feeling that everyone was strung up as tight a I was except for Chambrun. He sat by the telephone where he just finished talking, and his lips were spread in a kind of Cheshire cat smile. I'd seen that look before when he was about to pull a rabbit out of his hat.

At her suggestion Mrs. Haven took Linda over to her penthouse, surrounded by three of Hardy's cops. There was no question of allowing Linda to go home unguarded now, and what was happening where we were now was police business. Four very unhappy-looking men were ushered into Chambrun's living room: the elevator operator and his cop partner and Jerry Dodd's security man and his cop partner who'd been guarding the fire stairs. I knew the two hotel people well, longtime and long-trusted employees.

Hardy laid it on the line to them. T.C. had attacked Linda up here on the roof. There was no way he could have gotten up here without riding the elevator or coming up the fire stairs. The four men all tried to answer at once. No way! Not possible!

The elevator operator, named Dick Welles, spelled out his position.

"No one just gets a ride up here with us, Lieutenant," he said. "No one's been brought up here who wasn't okayed by you or Sergeant Lawson. We brought you all up here a few minutes ago, and the last trip before that we brought up the girl and Sergeant Lawson. Before that Mr. Haskell. That's been it for hours."

His cop partner agreed. "Nobody else up or down, Lieutenant," he said.

The two who'd been on the fire stairs were equally positive. No one at all had come or gone their way. Somehow you couldn't listen to these four guys, each assigned to a stranger to work with, and imagine some kind of a sell-out. It just didn't make sense.

Hardy, up a dead-end street, wasn't about to throw in the towel. "He could have been up here before we put the double watch on," he said. "That was after Haskell was attacked last night and brought up here." The lieutenant played his last card. "We've been convinced all along that T.C. is working for someone else. You want to come clean, Mr. Nelson?" He faced the singer. "Our anonymous caller has been trying to tell us all along that you were it. We've thought it was a gag. But you could have been hiding T.C. since last night!"

"Are you out of your effing mind?" Mancuso shouted at him.

"Keep it down, Buster," Lawson said. He was standing right next to Stan Nelson's bodyguard.

"Maybe you better hand over that gun of yours to me."

"This is absurd, Lieutenant," Stan said. "I haven't hired anyone to do anything for me, except Butch and Johnny who are always with me. Are you still dreaming I had something against Nora Sands, hired someone to polish off her son and her? Whoever your anonymous friend is, he's been trying to get you to look the other way, away from him. A child could read that maneuver if he had the wit to think at all."

"You want to charge us with something, get to it," Johnny Floyd said. "If not, we're getting the hell out of here. We don't have to put up with this baloney!"

"I think you'd better have some sort of evidence, Lieutenant," Stan said quietly. "Johnny's right. We don't have to put up with this, you know."

The phone interrupted this exchange. Chambrun, sitting next to it, answered. "Thanks, Jerry," he said. "Tell the new crew on the elevator to bring him up here." He put down the phone and gave Hardy that same secret smile. "It's my turn to go fishing, Walter," he said. "I hope I get something more solid on my hook than you have."

"What are you talking about?" Hardy said.

"We're about to have a chance to try my best guess on for size," Chambrun said. He got up from his chair and walked over to the front door. "Let me play it my way, Walter." He opened the door and stood looking at the elevator alcove. I could see the indicator light blinking over the elevator door as the car came up from the lobby. It seemed to take forever. Finally the car reached the roof, the door slipped open, and the Reverend Leonard Martin stepped out into the clear.

"Oh, there you are, Mr. Chambrun," he said. "I got your message that arrangements have been made for Nora's funeral."

"Come in," Chambrun said.

Martin walked in and stopped, obviously puzzled at finding a crowd there. Chambrun came in behind him and closed the door. "My message, Martin, was that arrangements had been made for a funeral, not Nora's funeral."

"I don't understand," Martin said.

"For your funeral, Mr. Martin, unless I'm very much mistaken," Chambrun said.

IT WAS CHAMBRUN'S old magician's trick. I've seen him pull it dozens of times—the rabbit out of the hat, the lady sawed in half who walks away all in one piece. There's a kind of irritating vanity that goes with it, but I find myself watching with my jaws hanging open like a country yokel, glancing around at others with that little-boy look of "my papa is smarter than your papa." I could see it coming, and Hardy could see it coming. The lieutenant had been there before and he was braced for it. Chambrun would come up with a bright idea, but it was the lieutenant who would have to prove it out, make it stand up.

The Reverend Martin didn't buckle under the first punch.

"I don't think I understand, Mr. Chambrun," he said. "My funeral?"

"Shall I tell you or will you tell me—how it all was from the start?" Chambrun asked.

Hardy must have given Sergeant Lawson some kind of signal, because the detective was suddenly directly behind Martin, giving him a quick frisk for a weapon. Martin twitched, like a girl being unexpectedly tickled.

"Really, Sergeant! What did you expect to find?" he asked.

Lawson just backed away, giving Hardy the sign that Martin was clean.

"I could have told the sergeant you wouldn't be armed, Martin," Chambrun said. "Your man, T.C., is your weapon, right?"

"I simply don't know what you're talking about," Martin said.

"Extraordinary consistency to T.C.'s patterns," Chambrun said, as though Martin hadn't spoken. "He evidently convinced himself a long time ago that it was safer to try that old magician's trick of misdirection rather than to stay silent and out of sight. These anonymous phone calls that have been plaguing the police and the press are an example. 'Don't look my way, look at Stan Nelson and his friends.' He's not unlike you, Reverend. 'I am against sin, I am on God's side. Look somewhere else.'"

"Are you suggesting that I—I?"

"I'm not suggesting, I'm charging you with hiring a man to commit murder for you, Martin," Chambrun said. "I repeat, shall I tell you how it is, or will you tell us?"

"I don't know this man T.C. you're talking about," Martin said.

"At least you will admit to a contact with you, because there is a witness—probably several witnesses," Chambrun said. "T.C., playing his twisted game again, gave you away. At the Private Lives Club, Reverend; T.C. came there to let you know something you needed to know. But he couldn't resist his passion for misdirection. He chucked you under the chin, insulted you, called you names and got himself thrown out. He thought he was telling the world that he had no contact with you, that he had nothing but contempt for you. Knowing his pattern, that settled things for me. That little drama was supposed to make us look somewhere else. All it does is make me keep looking at you, Martin."

"If that man who made a scene with me at the Private Lives Club is your T.C.," Martin said, "then, yes, I did, of course, see him. But that is the only time I—"

"There isn't time for useless denials," Chambrun said. "I will tell you, then, how it was. For a long time you've needed protection from people your New Morality crusade was attacking, people in the world of pornography who wanted you off their backs. You hired a man named Tom Colson to fill that role for you. It doesn't matter much where you found him. Maybe he came to you. He has some kind of perverted hatred for professional prostitutes. He demonstrated that here in the hotel when he worked for me. He was just the kind of monster you needed, Reverend.''

"This is preposterous!'' Martin said.

"Your trouble, Martin, is that you cannot really read people. They are black or white to you. You talk about what an extraordinary woman Nora Sands was, but, really, she was just an attractive whore to you. Too attractive, because in the end she tempted you to—how shall I say it?—to fall off the wagon. You had a sexual passage with her.''

"No!'' Little beads of sweat had broken out on Martin's forehead. "I tell you, Chambrun—''

"I'm telling you,'' Chambrun said. "It amused Nora to persuade you to dive off your sanctimonious platform. But she was extraordinary, a fact you didn't really understand at all. She didn't do it to set you up for Zach Thompson's blackmail factory. That wasn't her style. It amused her to prove to herself that sexual pleasure was stronger than all your high-sounding moral pronouncements. That's all she wanted, and you showed her she was right.''

"This simply isn't—''

"Oh, yes it is, Martin. The tragedy is that you couldn't understand why it had happened to you. You could only think that her next move would be to expose you, make the New Morality a laughing stock, put an end to your crusade—which, I'll concede, may be genuine enough.''

In that crowded room you could have heard a pin drop except for the voices of the two men. There was a fascination in watching the Reverend Martin begin to crumble.

"I don't know where your night of delight took place," Chambrun said. "Perhaps I should say 'morning of delight' because Nora wouldn't have taken you anywhere until after the club closed. I suppose it was to one of Zach Thompson's places. She wouldn't have taken you to her apartment because the boy, Eddie, was there. So you assumed, when your 'sinning' was over, that she had evidence that would destroy you, perhaps pictures, perhaps a sound tape. She didn't have, because, as I say, that wasn't her style. But you had to make sure, and T.C. was more than willing to help you."

Martin opened his mouth as if he wanted to keep protesting, but no sound came out. He was a man looking back at a nightmare.

"Friday night, when you knew Nora was at work, you and T.C. went to her apartment. T.C. is a genius with locks, I suspect. You got into her apartment and you began to look for the 'evidence' you were sure she had. You hadn't done enough research on the boy's habits, unfortunately. That night he had lost his key, and he came up the fire escape to get in, and you and T.C. were there. Perhaps he listened to you talking, perhaps you were threatening to silence Nora. That would be T.C.'s way of thinking. The boy heard, started to get away to warn his mother, made some kind of sound you heard. T.C. ran down inside the house, ran around the outside of the alley, and caught up with Eddie Sands as he climbed off the fire escape.

Maybe the boy shouted some kind of threat at him, or maybe he just opened his mouth to yell for help. Whichever, T.C. shot him in the face.''

Martin made a gesture with his manicured hands like someone warding off a swarm of bees.

''You are just coming up behind T.C. in the alley when this happens. What to do? When the boy is found every contact of Nora's will be questioned. You, who have been spending night after night at the Private Lives Club in her company, are bound to be questioned. The devious mind of T.C. came up with a better answer. The boy's body could be planted so that someone else who had been closely involved with Nora would be involved. Stan Nelson was a perfect target. T.C. felt he could plant the body here, he knew the hotel as if it was his own home. I suspect the boy's body was put in his car—or yours, Reverend. T.C. came here, went up to the Health Club where an old friend of his was on the evening shift. He sold Tony Camargo on something—perhaps that he could clear himself of the old charge. Tony left T.C. alone in the office and the impression of the keys was taken. T.C. had no reason to suppose his name had been put on the clipboard sheet. First misstep. He goes down to the telethon in the ballroom where the place is crowded with hundreds of screamers. He gets Stan to autograph one of those green pledge cards. Stan doesn't pay much attention to those autograph seekers, but if he had looked right at T.C. it wouldn't have meant anything to him.''

"Not even Haskell's drawing meant anything," Stan said.

"So T.C. got his keys made, planted the autographed card on the boy's body, waited his time. Maybe he had the body in the laundry bag or hamper, moved it into the rear service elevator and up to the Health Club on the service elevator, dumped the body in the pool, and walked away from the whole thing. When Carl Hulman found the body the next morning, and T.C. knew exactly when that would be, the anonymous phone calls began. Who else but T.C.?

"Time passes. The next thing T.C. had to do was get back into Nora's apartment to find the evidence you hadn't discovered the night before. But he had to wait to silence Tony Camargo first. He knew how Tony came and went, waited for him at the basement loading platform, and finished him off. Then he raced back downtown to search Nora's apartment. Unfortunately for her she came home before he was finished. He was onto violence in high gear. He beat her unconscious. He meant to kill her, but he had to leave before he was sure. Perhaps there'd been enough noise to rouse people in the building. He gets in touch with you, Reverend, and you go to Jane Street. You 'find' Nora knowing that you will find her. You play the role of honest citizen and call the police. Nora is taken to St. Vincent's. T.C. has to be sure, he goes there too, and finds himself sitting right across from Mark Haskell in the waiting room. Mark should know him, but apparently doesn't. T.C. takes off when Mark goes to the phone, but he knows Mark will remember, sooner or later. He hides in the linen closet on the second floor of this hotel, knowing Mark will come to his apartment sooner or later. When he does, T.C. attacks him. Fortunately Alec Watson turned up at the crucial moment. Have I left something out, Mr. Martin?"

Martin stared, almost blankly, at the Man.

"What was he doing up here on the roof tonight?" Hardy asked.

"Safest place for him to hide," Chambrun said. "Since we thought there was no way he could get up here no one would look for him here. He's never left the hotel since he attacked Mark last night. Couldn't risk it. We had the whole place covered like a tent."

"You—you cannot prove one word of this fantasy, Mr. Chambrun," Martin said, in a shaken voice.

Chambrun gave him a sardonic smile. "I don't have to prove it, Mr. Martin. That's Lieutenant Hardy's job. But since it's the only story that will fit all the facts, it will prove out in time. T.C. may be helpful when we talk to him, however."

"If we talk to him," Hardy said.

"We'll talk to him, Walter," Chambrun said. "He can't have left the hotel. Every possible exit is covered. He came up here by way of the elevator and he left that way."

"No sir, Mr. Chambrun!" Welles, the elevator operator, cried out. "He never rode the elevator, I swear to that!"

"I said 'by way of the elevator,' Dick; I didn't say *in* the elevator. He knew, from working here, that the doors on each floor can be opened from inside the shaft. He rode the roof of the car. When it came up here he clung to grillwork inside the shaft. When the car went down he let himself into the elevator alcove. But he had bad luck. He walked right into Linda Zazkowski. She screams loud enough to wake the dead. He had to get safe in a hurry after he slugged her, and so he climbed back into the shaft. He's gone down somewhere into the hotel by now. He'll be found, Walter. It may take time, but he'll be found. I suggest a quick search of the Health Club."

"It's been searched and locked up," Sergeant Lawson said.

"Do I have to remind you, Sergeant, that T.C. has keys to those locks?" Chambrun said. "Now, I've got a hotel to run and Mark has to get the press off our backs."

Chambrun was the Cheshire cat again, and I followed him out of the elevator alcove.

"It had to be Martin," Chambrun said, as we waited for the elevator. "Nelson and Company would never have made those anonymous telephone calls drawing attention to themselves. Zachary Thompson is a creep, but a very shrewd creep. He would never hire a psycho like T.C. to work for him. His business is too touchy, too delicately balanced. It had to be Martin, who just didn't read Nora Sands correctly. Poor girl, she finally paid in spades for her fun."

The elevator arrived, with a relief operator and a relief cop as its crew. We started down for the second floor.

"Can Hardy prove out your theory?" I asked.

"Trust Walter," Chambrun said. "He'll find the car in which Eddie Sands' body was carried from Jane Street to the Beaumont. There will be blood in it. The poor kid bled his life away! He'll find the bullet that killed Eddie in the alley between houses on Jane Street. He'll find the place in which Martin was tempted to lose his virginity. Too bad, since he couldn't resist temptation, he couldn't have enjoyed it—instead of starting T.C. on a murder spree."

We left the elevator at the second floor and headed for Chambrun's office. I remember glancing over my shoulder at the linen room. The last time I'd passed it someone had been waiting there for me. I found myself walking very close to Chambrun.

Chambrun turned the knob on his office door and found it locked. He looked irritated.

"Ruysdale is supposed to be here," he said.

The handsome Miss Ruysdale was rarely not where he expected her to be. He found his office key and opened the door. Miss Ruysdale's office was brightly lighted, but no Miss Ruysdale.

Chambrun walked briskly to the door of his own office, opened it, and came to such an abrupt stop that I actually bumped into him from behind. I started to turn back but I was stopped by a voice inside the office.

"Don't try, Haskell, if you want the lady to have a head that works!"

Miss Ruysdale was sitting in a chair, facing the doorway in which he stood. A wide piece of adhesive tape was fastened across her mouth. Her hands were apparently tied behind the back of the chair. I saw shapely ankles tied to its front legs. Betsy Ruysdale was trussed up like a Thanksgiving turkey, and standing just behind her, baseball cap pushed back on his head, was T.C. He was holding what looked like a cannon to the lady's head.

"Second safest place in the hotel," T.C. said, his teeth bared in that arrogant smile. "Plus I need your help, Chambrun."

"Help?"

"To get out of this labyrinth, of course," T.C. said. "You're the one person who can provide me with a one-way street to safety. I know how precious this babe is to you, friend. It didn't take me long when I worked here to find out where you spend your leisure time, and what kind of leisure it is!" He laughed.

"How do you expect me to go about it?" Chambrun asked.

"You're the one with the answers to that," T.C. said. "It better be quick and clean, because the lady will go with me until I'm satisfied there are no tricks."

Miss Ruysdale's eyes swiveled from Chambrun to me and back again.

"If I'm going to be any use to you, Colson, I've got to get to the phones on my desk," Chambrun said, sounding quite casual.

"Help yourself," T.C. said, "only keep your hands in sight. No opening drawers, no reaching for a weapon you may have hidden there."

Chambrun, hands held out in front of him in plain view, moved noiselessly across the thick Oriental rug to his desk. He sat down, reached automatically for a cigarette in the silver box there, held his desk lighter to it, and leaned back, his eyes narrowed against the smoke.

"A car in the basement garage," he suggested to T.C. "A man to drive you wherever you want to go."

"I'll do the driving," T.C. said. "There are two ways to do this, you know, Chambrun. You can play it cute and try to sneak us out. Or you can tell the world I'm going, with a gun at this lady's head, and let them watch. That might be the safest. No one will make a wrong move if they know what the score is. You can make it clear to them that the doll here will be no use to you with a hole in her head."

I tried swallowing to get the taste of ashes out of my mouth. This crazy psycho would do just what he threatened to do, I hadn't a doubt of that.

"First I'll make arrangements for a car," Chambrun said. "Then I'll have to contact Homicide and my security people and warn them off."

"So start in," T.C. said.

Chambrun picked up the phone on his desk and dialed an extension. "Hello, Benson? I want a car available, gassed up for a trip.... In ten minutes if you can make it.... Thank you."

Someone coughed. I thought it was T.C., but he was looking straight at me. I turned my head and there was Jerry Dodd, our security chief, standing in the door to Chambrun's private rest room. T.C. spun around. It was so fast I almost didn't believe it. Jerry shot T.C. once in the arm, once in the midsection. I'd made a dive for the floor, but I thought I heard T.C.'s gun drop with a thud.

I scrambled up and Chambrun was handing me a sharp-edged letter opener from his desk.

"Her hands," he said to me.

T.C. was lying on the rug, his face twisted into a mask of agony, one arm shattered, the other hugging his stomach. Jerry Dodd was standing over him, gun ready to fire again if he had to. Chambrun was kneeling in front of Betsy Ruysdale.

"This is going to hurt, luv," he said very gently. "One quick pull."

Then he ripped the adhesive strip away from her mouth. At the same moment I sliced the cord that was tying her hands behind her back.

"Pierre!" I heard her whisper.

He held his face against her cheek for a moment. If I'd ever had any doubts about them they were dispelled in that moment. I glanced at Jerry Dodd.

"You got some kind of crystal ball somewhere?" I asked him.

"Not exactly," he said, never taking his eyes off the moaning T.C. "Under the boss's desk is an electric button—like your mother used to have under the dining room table to let the butler know he could take the soup dishes. When he steps on that button it sets off an alarm in my office that spells big trouble. Back way in. He keeps the door oiled."

Chambrun stood with his arm around Ruysdale's shoulders. She was still trying to get herself pulled together.

"I hope you left him alive enough to talk," he said to Jerry. "That will help Hardy wrap this up."

Jerry looked up and gave the Man a tight smile. "One inch below the heart and two inches to the left," he said. "You know me, boss, I always know what I'm doing."

"I'm very grateful to you, friend," Chambrun said.

He never forgets to bestow a medal when it's earned.

DEADLY PROMISE

MIGNON F. BALLARD

You'd better watch out,
You'd better not cry,
Or there's no doubt
You're the next one to die...

The first victim was her husband. Then his best friend. So Molly
Stonehouse had come to Harmony, Georgia, for Christmas—to
discover who in her husband's cheery hometown was a murderer.

At the center of the mystery is a secret from the past, an innocent,
boyish prank that, decades later, is unfolding with deadly
precision.

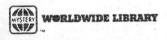

HAL'S OWN MURDER CASE
LEE MARTIN

LABOR PAINS

Two weeks away from the birth of her baby, Ft. Worth detective
Deb Ralston decided her sixteen-year-old son, Hal, had picked a rotten
time to hitchhike halfway across the state with his girlfriend, Lorie, and be
arrested for murder.

The victim, a young woman, had been hacked with Hal's hunting knife
and left in Lorie's sleeping bag. Now Lorie is missing and Hal's in jail.

Ralston hits the tiny East Texas town in her official capacity as worried
mother—a role that quickly expands into investigating officer. The trail
leads to places of the heart no mother-to-be wants to go...but with a cop's
unerring instinct, she follows the ugly path into the twisted mind of a
ruthless killer.

NIGHT WALKER

JEAN HAGER

GRAHAM THORNTON DESERVED TO DIE

At least, according to anyone with a good reason to kill the wealthy, arrogant owner of the new resort lodge in Buckskin, Oklahoma. And that meant just about everybody.

The lodge had been built on an Indian graveyard, and the Indian employees are convinced Thornton's murder is the vengeful act of a night walker, a Cherokee witch. Chief Mitch Bushyhead, however, believes whoever tampered with Thornton's insulin was very human. His list of suspects seems endless: a vindictive ex-wife; a hateful sister; the lover Thornton was blackmailing.

Then a second murder leads Bushyhead into a web of secrets, lies and hidden depravations...and a killer's desperate final act that leads perilously close to home.

Flight to
YESTERDAY
VELDA JOHNSTON

A NIGHTMARE REVISITED

Dubbed a "young Jean Harris" by the press, Sara Hargreaves spent four years in prison for a crime of passion she didn't commit. Now she's escaped, and she's desperate to clear her name and to see her dying mother.

As her face appears nightly on the local news, Sara disguises herself, and with the help of a young law student she is forced to trust, she returns to the scene of the crime.

The fashionable sanatorium where handsome plastic surgeon Dr. Manuelo Covarrubias was stabbed with a knife bearing Sara's fingerprints looks much the same. But as Sara begins her flight to yesterday, the secrets surrounding the callous playboy doctor who jilted her unfold. Secrets that once drove someone to murder...secrets that could kill again.

 **WORLDWIDE LIBRARY**
™

BACKLASH
PAULA GOSLING

Winner of the John Creasey Award for crime fiction

THE TASK THAT FACED GENERAL HOMICIDE SEEMED MONUMENTAL

They had four dead cops from four different precincts, all shot through the head. The headlines were screaming cop killer. Rookies were making sudden career changes, while veterans of the force were anxiously eyeing retirement dates. Panic was growing.

For Lieutenant Jack Stryker, the pressure was coming everywhere: up from below, down from above, and in from the outside. And with each new death, the pressure increased. Was the killer shooting cops at random...or was there a more sinister reason for the murders?

But when Stryker is hit and his partner is almost fatally wounded...Stryker knows it's time to forget procedure and put an end to open season on Grantham's finest...before he becomes the next trophy of a demented killer.

"Gosling's novels have all met with critical acclaim."

— *Library Journal*